ACCIDENTAL *Proposal*

Accidental Lovers
Book 2

Y. M. NELSON

ONE CREATIVE SUMMER PRESS

Charlotte, NC

This book contains adult content and contains a few scenes and mentions that may trigger some people. For a list of these triggers go to:
https://ymnelson.com/books/trigger-warnings/#accidental

To the readers that believe love persists,
despite the prejudice, ignorance, and negativity
that threaten its downfall.

Also By Y. M. Nelson

The Owen & Makayla Trilogy
Secret Second Chances, an Owen and Makayla Retelling
Accidental Lovers Series
The Accidental Swipe
The Accidental Proposal
The On Purpose Wedding (coming soon)

Standalone Novels
The One You Slept On (coming soon)
The Undesirables (coming soon)

Short Stories
"Introverted"
(featured in *North Carolina's Emerging Writers: An Anthology of Fiction*)

One

Jason

*B*UZZ, BUZZ, BUZZ.

    Jason's phone buzzed so much that it threatened to fall off the nightstand.

"Would you get that already?" Fortune demanded, eyes closed, lying on her back.

Jason forced himself to turn away from her and grabbed his phone as it bounced off the nightstand's edge. He wanted to silence it and put it back, but the long line of text messages from Graham made him pause.

8:03 PM, yesterday

> Waiting on you again

9:54 PM, yesterday

> Where are you, you didn't say you weren't coming

7:49 AM

> I'm headed to your house with a couple of cops.

When had Graham become such a nag?

"Who was it?" Fortune asked.

"Just Graham."

"Well, answer him."

"It's already over. Not important."

"He's your best friend. Whatever it is, it's important enough for him to text at the crack of dawn on a Saturday. Answer it. Trust that I'm never ignoring Louis or Celeste for you."

So, everyone was chiming in on his life. "Okay. Fine. I'll text him."

"Thank you."

Fortune sighed, sounding exasperated, though she didn't move. She was in that half-spent, half-zen place she usually got to after they made love. It was the moment he could talk her into going again.

And Graham was spoiling that moment.

Jason sent a quick text to Graham, calling off the cavalry, but he knew that wouldn't be the end of it. Jason had done the unthinkable—he'd ghosted the guys for a girl. At some point today, he'd have to answer for his crime and see his best friend in person.

He'd been putting off seeing any of the guys since getting together with Fortune. What had it been? Three months? The longest they'd gone without hanging out. But who wanted to hang out with a buddy when sexy Fortune was around?

With a simple text, he possibly could've avoided them for another three months. But last night, he'd ghosted instead of just flaking, and they were going to want to know the cause. Which meant everyone would have to meet. For real this time. Time to get back to reality.

In a few minutes.

He twirled one of her short auburn curls around his pinky. The curl slid across his skin like silk. At the root, it was a rich sienna brown, which he was a little excited about. He wished she'd let it grow, so he'd have more of the luscious curls to run his fingers through. But she liked it short. He was simply happy she let him play in it because, evidently, not all Black women wanted you to touch their hair. It was so soft, like everything else in Fortune's bed—her sheets, her mattress, her.

Usually, she kept her curls wrapped up in some kind of headscarf at night, but right now, in a post-coital haze, her top half was completely uncovered, and the bedsheet draped over both of them barely covered her hips. He loved seeing her like this—naked, her medium brown skin like a piece of finished cherry wood, with swirls of darker brown in places. The sight of it awakened the creative spirit in him—the need to get his hands on something to hone it and bring out its beauty. Her skin begged to be touched, and he did. He couldn't stop when she was like this.

Come to think of it, where *was* her scarf thing? He searched among the sheets and found the scrap of satin fabric underneath her shoulder, near where he'd pushed it off so he could get his fingers in her hair while they made love.

He slid the head covering under his pillow. He wasn't hiding it; he just wanted to get it out of the way. If she never found it again, that might be okay with him.

"Speaking of friends, you know you need to meet mine."

"I've already met your friends. It didn't go well, remember?"

"Yes, of course, I remember."

Who could forget the night all four of them met for the first time? Jason had spotted Fortune on a date with his best bud, Graham. A date she swore she'd never go on. When they all saw each other, disaster struck, ending with Graham breaking Jason and Seth apart during an all-out brawl in The Graveyard's—the guys' favorite bar's—parking lot, and Jason and Fortune almost didn't get together.

After a hot night with her and a couple of emotional conversations afterwards, he'd had to make a decision: leave Fortune, or get to know her and take some time away from the gang to do so. So, he chose Fortune. He could use a break from the gang. They'd understand. After all, they'd been back and forth with each other for over twenty years.

He rationalized that his pursuit of Fortune took precedence over the guys, but he couldn't avoid them anymore. "That's why you need to meet them again. Erase the bad first impressions and all. They're better guys than that, I promise."

He leaned against her–his front against her side with one of his legs draped over hers–and breathed her intoxicating vanilla scent. Her eyes were still closed, so he took the moment to get his visual fill of her. His gaze lingered, taking in the fullness of her lips, the curve of her throat, the ampleness of her breasts.

"Why are you harshing my buzz?" She folded her arms over her chest. "And stop staring at my boobs."

"I wasn't staring!"

He laughed. He'd definitely been staring. Who could blame him? They were perfect.

"Yes, you were. I could feel it."

"So, what if I was?" He reached his hand under her folded arms and nudged them loose. "And you haven't felt anything yet." He cupped a breast while he licked and kissed her neck.

She playfully pushed him away but quickly succumbed to his seduction and arched to him, pushing more of her breast into his hand.

As he kissed his way down her body, her hums and moans were a drug he couldn't live without. He fondled her nipple until it became a hard bud. Then he moved to the other to hear more of that sensual melody. He drank in her rich vanilla buttery scent, nuzzling deeper and drowning in Fortune. She was so damned sexy when she was being no-nonsense. Thank goodness he didn't have anywhere to be that day.

Nope, that wasn't correct. He remembered Graham's frantic texts, and his own hastily typed response:

Forgot to tell you I got held up and couldn't come. Come by the house later. I'll text you.

He had to pull himself away from Fortune and get back to his life.

Get a hold of yourself, Reed.

He leaned away from her and took a few gulps of air, clearing the heady fog of laziness and lust. Slowly, his memory returned. He was asking her something, and ... He looked at her, and this time their gaze connected.

An innocent expression lit her face. A fake innocent expression.

His brows furrowed.

"What?" she asked.

He countered with a classic detective stare. "You lured me right in and made me forget what I was asking."

"I did no such thing." Sugar almost dripped from her lips when she smiled.

"You're like a pot of honey. But you're still avoiding the issue. Sweetie, these are my friends. You've got to meet them. Properly this time. I don't want them to think you're my secret." He moved his hands from her breasts and circled her waist protectively, hoping she recognized he wanted her in his life, not only in her bed. "And I don't want you to think that either, especially after that Mike guy."

"His name was Marshall, and ... yuck. I don't think that." Her tone was light, but her smile disappeared. She grew rigid under him, the soft compliance of her body gone in an instant.

He shouldn't have mentioned Marshall.

"Why?" she continued. "They already hate me. No need to remind them."

"They do not hate you!" He gave her a brief squeeze. "They just need to get to know you. And you haven't even met all of them. Ranjan wasn't at The Graveyard that night. I think you'd like him." Jason remembered his and Fortune's first conversation online when she mentioned accents. "He's the one with the British accent."

"So, *he's* the one I should have fallen in love with." Her lips parted in a wide grin.

"No. That would have been doomed from the start. He's not into girls."

"Hmm, okay. Seems I'll have to settle for you, then."

"Guess so." He trailed his index finger along the bridge of her nose. "Oh, yeah, and 'harshing your buzz'?" He raised one eyebrow. "Reclaim that from the nineties, did you?"

She shrugged. "Whatevs, man. I say what I want."

"Hmm. Does that mean I get to do what I want?"

He kissed her behind her ear and licked a path along her jaw to her chin.

Her sigh came out like a moan, and she shifted away. "As fun as that would be, I need to meet Louis for some errands this morning."

"Tell me you'll meet my friends, or I'm not letting you leave." He continued his pleasure journey, kissing his way from the tip of her chin to the hollow of her throat.

She laughed and squirmed and wriggled until he was forced to stop kissing, lest he get an accidental elbow to the stomach. She pushed her lips into a sexy pout that made him want to kiss them, but he waited for her response.

"Fine."

"You know that could've backfired on you."

She grabbed an empty box from the nightstand and dropped it on him.

He released her to avoid getting hit with it.

"We're out of condoms, so you get your wish. I'll meet your friends."

She slid from under him and made her way to the shower.

Clutching the empty prophylactics box, he felt cold without her heat, but the view as she walked to the bathroom was heavenly. He would settle for that view every morning.

"And stop staring at my ass!" she yelled before she closed the door.

Two

Jason

LEAVING FORTUNE'S HOUSE WAS painful, but it had to be done. He'd been going to her house straight from the job site for at least a week, ever since they became exclusive. If he had a hard day at work, he'd come over unless she had a work function. As a construction manager, his day rarely went past four, but hers as a seminar creator at a marketing firm, sometimes spilled into the evening. If a client had a soirée or if Fortune had to attend an after-work event, she wouldn't get home until after ten.

But the past week had been event-free for her and especially difficult for him, so he'd arrive at her door by 4:45 every evening, dusty, aching, and craving her. He hadn't been in his condo since last Sunday. The pile of mail beside his front door would need sorting, clothes would need laundering, and his fridge would need food. Of course, that meant stopping by the local brewery for his favorite IPA, then going home and calling Graham over and stomping him in *Mortal Kombat.* He'd threatened to storm Jason's house with a police brigade, so a video game stomping was warranted.

The entire way home, Jason thought about Fortune stalking like a model, stark naked in the daylight, to her bathroom. Three months ago, she'd never have done that, instead searching for something voluminous to cover herself. In that short span of time, she'd gone from unsure to confident, and all he'd done was love her. And he did love her. He loved everything about her, from her luscious mouth to those notches at her waist that were just big enough for his hands.

But he wasn't sure his friends would love her.

Ranjan would; Jason was sure of that because he was the sanest and most charming of them. The guys Ranjan dated always fell head over heels, some even before he could remember their last names. He was delightful, and so was Fortune. They would click right away.

Graham thought she was cute and appropriately humble obviously, or his big ego wouldn't have gone out with her. Jason wished a few of those punches he'd thrown that night had landed on Graham's face. But Jason and Fortune's date wouldn't have happened if he'd told Graham about her. It was Graham's ego—no one could get past it.

At least Graham wasn't as bad as Seth. If Jason were honest with himself, Seth was the reason Jason had put distance between Fortune and the group. When Seth and Graham met Fortune, chaos converged. Graham's date with her had been tanking fast, and Seth recognized her as "the woman who kneed me in the nuts." Graham stayed civil in the uncomfortable situation, but Seth added insult to injury by outing the way Jason had ended up on the online dating site that matched them. And when Seth doubled down on the insult that caused Fortune to knee him, Jason punched Seth, got them kicked out of The Graveyard, and knocked out his longtime friend.

That was the last time Jason had been to the bar or seen his friends in person.

Ever since, he'd avoided Graham's invites, and Graham complained about it. After every "not going to make it" text from Jason came dozens of Graham's responses asking why, mildly cursing him out, and now threatening to call the law and file a missing person report. Twenty–plus years of friendship and Graham's ego was too big to realize his best friend was mad, and Jason's emotions were too sensitive to not be petty. Maybe Fortune had the right idea to avoid them for as long as they could.

But he was over that now. Mostly.

As Jason exited the car and headed for his condo, his neighbor, Mrs. Kosinski, stopped him. "Well, hello! Are you new here?"

If this woman didn't know every way to needle him, he was a Martian. But with her round face adorned with thick glasses and her shock-white hair pulled back in a tight bun like an old-time school marm, she was adorable. That shedding little dog of hers she was holding under her arm was a level-ten miscreant, though.

"Hello, Mrs. Kosinski. It's me, Jason. From next door?" he greeted her as he scooped some mail that hadn't made it to the mailbox beside his front door.

"Yes, I quite well know who you are. And I also know that you haven't been here in so long the mail carrier decided to fling your bills and encrypted spy letters all over the complex. Why didn't you have your mail stopped if you were out of town?"

"Mrs. Kosinski, you know I'm not a spy. I helped you pick out your kitchen finishes for goodness sakes! And no, I wasn't out of town. I was at my girlfriend's place for a few days."

She brightened, her face wrinkling as she smiled. "Oh! That delightful woman that made you get a new plant?"

"I believe you also said something about my plant." He glanced at the flowerpot on the porch, which was now empty since he'd repotted the plant and moved it inside. "But yes, her name's Fortune."

"Yes, I did. It was bringing down my property value. In any case, I'm glad you're still with this Fortune. She's really bringing you good luck." She shifted the long-haired terror to her other arm when a sedan pulled up. "See how I did that?" she called as she walked to the waiting car—probably one of her kids taking her on errands.

A grandma telling dad jokes. Jason laughed and shook his head as he unlocked the door.

She'd been right about Fortune. His life was just better with her in it. Having her to come home to this week had been amazing. It had been a long time since he'd last felt this close, this excited about being with someone. He'd taken a step back from his other relationships to get to know her better.

Selfishly, Jason wanted Fortune all to himself—no nosy family members asking questions, no jeering friends making dirty jokes and vying to become enemies in the process—and for three months, he'd had her. She'd been the only thing occupying his time outside of his full-time job managing a dusty construction site and his part-time job corralling a classroom of teenagers and keeping them from dangerous shop equipment.

He did miss hanging out with the guys. But because Seth was such a wildcard, Jason avoided telling any of them that he'd worked things out with Fortune and that they were together. Which meant avoiding drunken nights at The Graveyard and gaming with his best bud.

Someone knocked at the door as soon as he put the IPAs in the fridge. Graham was earlier than Jason thought. His buddy must have raced over.

As he entered, Graham's face had a pinched look that only appeared when he was being extra judgy. Or it could be constipation. Since neither condition was pleasant, Jason decided not to ask and handed his best friend a game controller instead.

"Hey, stranger." Graham sounded like someone's grandfather attempting to make his grandson feel guilty about not coming around. "Where have you been?"

"And hello to you, too, Grandpa Reynolds."

Graham stared at him blankly.

About a month into Fortune and Jason's relationship, Graham had texted that Jason should have gotten over his breakup by now and come back to their Graveyard meet-ups. Jason hadn't even bothered to set the story straight—he would tell them the next time he saw them, and until then, he'd just avoid every get-together when he was invited.

But he couldn't do that any longer. He'd have to break it to his friends that he and Fortune were indeed together. Getting Graham back on his side and endorsing a group meeting was the next step.

Splitting into two people would be an easier task.

Jason sighed. "So, we're doing this now?"

Graham sunk into Jason's sofa, his stare still harsh and laser-focused. "I'm getting an explanation before you can deflect and distract with video games."

"Dude, it's just The Graveyard. It's not anybody's wedding or funeral or anything."

They both knew that their hangouts at The Graveyard weren't just hangouts. They were meetings of the minds, life-saving conclaves, fonts for life refreshment. Every other Friday, they took Lyfts to the sports bar that was nothing like a graveyard, drank themselves to excess while extolling the virtues or venting the complaints of life, and disbanded with the understanding that no one would call or text anyone else until at least noon the next day, no matter what was said. It was at one of these hangouts that Seth dared Jason to find someone on SwipeMatch, the body-positive plus-size online dating app where he'd found Fortune.

Jason had missed several of these holy drunken moments—along with a handful of other significantly less important random events—and that was evidently more than enough for a threat of police intervention.

"I've been working," Jason mused, throwing his friend an equally withering but smug look. "And having fun. A lot of fun."

"Without me? I thought we were bros. And the best prankster duo in Charlotte, I might add."

Jason laughed. "Not that kind of fun. Naked fun with a woman."

"Who is it this time? Having secret dates with Rogue Storm?" Graham's eyebrows rose almost to his hairline as he mentioned the famous plus-size pop star who always wore next to nothing onstage. He struggled not to smile.

Jason punched Graham in the shoulder, and the controller fell out of Graham's hand. "Dude. Not an insult. Rogue Storm's hot." He paused from getting the second controller to think. "Hmm. And half-naked most of the time. But no, not her. Fortune."

Graham reached for his controller, but stopped when Jason mentioned her name. "Fortune? I thought you broke up with her after the ... you know the—"

"You mean the hate sex? You're a grown man, and you can't say the word *sex*? What is with you today?"

"I'm trying not to come off like Seth." Graham shook his head. "I'm tripping."

And there it was. Jason thought he'd get through at least one round of *Mortal Kombat* before this piano dropped.

Yet, after only a few minutes, Seth was making conversation between Jason and Graham awkward, and the guy wasn't even in the room. Seth, the loudmouth and general killjoy of every hangout.

Jason sighed heavily and slumped over, elbows on knees, with his hands over his face, scrubbing at his little more than a five o'clock shadow. Beating Seth up had been letting him off the hook. Jason should have talked with Seth extensively about his rudeness. But when he had to choose between hashing it out with Seth and hanging out with Fortune in her soft-as-a-cloud bed, Jason would pick Fortune every time.

Why they'd even put up with Seth for this long was beyond Jason. Seth was the reason that this whole thing had happened—for good and for bad. It wasn't lost on Jason how ironic the whole situation was. Seth's negativity, in a way, had brought Jason and Fortune together. If Seth's aversion to plus-size women hadn't forced Jason into a truth-or-dare game, he wouldn't have found Fortune's profile in the first place. And Seth insulting her at Silver Foxes only compelled her to use her SwipeMatch profile to find someone for her best friend Louis's gala. To find Jason.

That same hatred and negativity had kept him from hanging out with his friends for three months.

Jason stared into space, rethinking what he'd been telling himself all this time—that he was taking a break from the gang to get to know Fortune. It was crap, and deep down, he knew it. Really, he'd been delaying the inevitable. Hanging out with his friends meant he'd have to confront Seth, come to an understanding, and arrange a proper meeting between

Fortune and all of them. That thought made him nauseated. Well, avoiding time was over.

"Jason?" Graham leaned forward to meet his best friend's stare.

Jason blinked and then agreed with Graham's earlier point. "Yeah, no one wants to come off like Seth."

"He's the reason you disappeared on us, isn't it? Why we haven't seen you in a year?"

Graham was hovering like a helicopter mom, making Jason squirm. They didn't do this come-to-Jesus emotional stuff. This was bro space. "It's only been three months."

"Still."

Jason snatched up both controllers and shoved one at Graham. "Just play the game."

He sat on the opposite end of the sofa and began the set-up sequence. As usual, he picked Scorpion, with one of the best finishing moves of all the game's characters.

Which, of course, meant Graham picked SubZero.

The characters were twins, and every time Graham chose SubZero, it needled Jason a tiny bit. Graham was saying subconsciously, "I'm just like you, and you can't beat me without beating yourself". Profound? Possibly. Would he ever share that with Graham? Never.

Still, Jason channeled Scorpion and took out his frustration on SubZero.

When "Finish him!" scrolled across the screen and echoed through the townhouse, Jason ended the flawless round with the lightning move.

"Felt good, huh?" Graham asked blandly.

Jason refused to look at his friend, staring at the TV instead. "Let's go again."

This time, Graham picked first and chose Johnny Cage. "So, you're with a woman Seth doesn't like. Who cares? Seth doesn't like a lot of things that make sense—recycling, affordable housing, and treating women with respect. Why does his opinion matter more than the rest of ours?"

"He doesn't even know her, and he called her a whale and a bitch? Why would I want to be around that while I'm dating this woman?" Jason frowned.

"I get it. But you know how to deal with Seth. Confront him—no fists, though—and let him know what's up. He usually calms down."

"I shouldn't even have to do that. If I introduce this woman as my girlfriend, he should at least respect that and be civil."

Graham paused the game and turned to Jason. "What if Seth never warms up to her or grows to like her? What then?"

Jason shook his head. "Fortune is amazing. He'll like her if he gives her a chance."

"You know how Seth can be—stubborn, always thinking his way is right. You've got to be prepared for what may happen if he doesn't think she's amazing."

Jason shook his head, banishing the thought that Seth's stubbornness was any match for Fortune's charisma. Seth had always been a jerk but never an all-out bully. "All I have to do is get him to see how great she is, and he'll be wowed.

I'm thinking dinner at Diamond Steak. We can all go. Ranjan can be a buffer as usual."

"That's an idea. Maybe we should bring dates, so she won't feel put on the spot," Graham offered. "I think I can get Dani onboard."

"So, you and Dani are back on again?"

Graham leaned away from Jason and focused more on the game. "We're working it out. We should be fine before it's time to pick a day."

Jason looked at his friend out of the corner of his eye. "Does she know you went on a date with Fortune?"

"One of the reasons we're getting back together. I told her it was so bad that it made me miss her and want her back."

The two laughed. Gaming with Graham, gossiping, and day drinking was a colossal waste of time, and Jason wondered how he went over three months without it. "You're a player of the highest caliber, dude."

Three

Jason

A FEW DAYS AFTER reuniting with his best friend, Jason dressed for work, still preoccupied with the group dinner he'd suggested. Fortune was more than a little apprehensive, but she'd agreed. "I'll be cool if you give me like two weeks. Don't schedule it for next weekend. I need some time for it to soak in."

Everyone else he'd talked to was on board, if halfheartedly, which was all he could really expect at this point. Everyone except Seth. He'd cave with a few more texts, though. Once the dinner rolled around, everyone would come together. If not, Jason would fix any problems.

His dad's disappointed glare flashed in his mind, and he did a double take.

It was the one thing he hadn't been able to fix—his father's disappointment at his choice of career, despite everything Jason had accomplished. Any time someone called him Mr.

Fix-it, or he resolved to fix something, his dad's face would revisit his memory.

He shook away the grim look flooding his thoughts and headed out to Beans & Bread for breakfast and a stop at the office. He glanced at the text his assistant Gabi had just sent:

> Architect made another change to hi-rise project. Need your sign-off.

He groaned and pulled out of his parking space, narrowly missing a morning biker in full protective gear, beginning his morning ride.

"Sorry, man," he yelled out the window as he drove off.

Despite the distractions, Jim Reed's face stayed at the forefront of Jason's thoughts and kept his optimism at bay. If only he'd gone to school closer to home, included his dad on the business side of things, even persuaded him to come to his graduation or his grand opening, his dad would see how great a construction manager Jason was and would approve.

He would not make that same mistake with Fortune and his friends; he wasn't going to hide her away just because she and Seth didn't get along. His friends needed to get to know her, and she needed to get to know them. They'd either love her or respect the fact that he did. Because he liked having Fortune in his life, and that life included those hooligans he called friends. That was how it should've happened with his dad. He should've told his dad everything about his career plans and begged him to see how well he was doing.

No. Stop dwelling, Reed. He went through this every time he was faced with problems, doubters, and general naysayers. He thought about the impasse with his dad and made it his goal to fix whatever it was.

This was not the way to start a day at the job. He opened the door to Beans & Bread and inhaled the rich decadence of ground coffee beans, cinnamon, and sugar, determined to banish the disappointment back to the far reaches of his consciousness where it belonged.

"Did you bring coffee?" Gabi asked by way of a greeting when Jason entered the office. She was a snarky redhead who wore glasses with huge frames and *Star Trek*-themed t-shirts, despite Jason's rule about no printed t-shirts unless they were company shirts. But she was an awesome assistant, so he gave up on the reprimands after she'd shown up one day with hot coffee, wearing a shirt that said "Energize" and had a picture of a cup of coffee mid-beam out.

Today's t-shirt had a headshot of a Black woman in uniform and the words "Let's Fly" on it with a ship in the background. The woman was striking and reminded him a bit of Fortune. Maybe he should start watching *Star Trek*.

He showcased the tray with four large steaming cups, then took one for himself before giving her the rest. With a greeting like that, she'd consume at least two of them before the morning was over. Everyone else who came in would have to settle for whatever pod coffee was in the breakroom.

"More changes to the exterior of the fourth floor. They are sure this can be done without compromising integrity."

"But are the inspectors sure?"

"They signed off." She pointed to their signatures, took a sip from her cup, and sighed. "I love the way caffeine zips through my veins. But Reed? I hate this project."

Loathing was creeping through him as well. They'd only been on site for a few months, and this commercial project was proving to be a pain.

After months of going back and forth with proposals, he'd won part of the downtown high-rise multi-use office and temporary housing project. It would keep his crew working steadily for at least a year, maybe two, if it panned out. Reed Reno & Construction won part of the initial block building before the steel framing went up, and some of the interior work at the end of the project, including designing and constructing an office space.

But with so-called assured work came a lot of headaches, especially when you had to deal with hotshot architects who wanted to be the next Frank Lloyd Wright, bent on designing art instead of functional space. Add to that, developers with big budgets but no concept of the cost of materials and labor, and you got headaches. Even Gabi had complained, and she hadn't been on site yet. The number of revisions alone had her working nonstop for weeks. And it seemed every morning she was sifting through emails and printing off AutoCAD drawings with changes.

They took the new drawings to the conference room, spread them on the table, and studied them in silence. Gabi was mostly waiting on his reaction and drinking.

The developer decided this week that he no longer wanted walls on three sides, opting for a weird design where everyone with certain corner offices on the top floors got not one window, but two walls of windows. So, they would have to demo half the work they'd erected the week before to create something that he wasn't sure was a sound plan. It was definitely less sturdy than the block walls from the previous plan. It didn't have to make sense to Jason; he just had to build it.

On top of that, it meant they'd have to shift to another job after the top floor demo so the steel framing crew could do their work. Gabi wouldn't be happy about that.

When he presented the revised plan to his team, most of them groaned and complained.

"We just finished that side!"

"Are they going to pay overtime when we get behind schedule?"

"This is just a waste."

"How are we going to even fix this?"

Austin Dvorzak, his longtime general contractor and project manager, was ever the optimist. "If anyone can rebuild a developer's dream, it's Reed. Boss, how we lookin'?"

Jason exhaled and glared from the plans to the half-framed building for a good minute before answering. He stared at the plans once more, and then stared at his team, his mind whirling with scenarios. About twenty men and women showed up today: most of them were full-timers on his payroll, a few were contractors, and a few more were day laborers that he'd have to keep far away from the majority of the demo, or OSHA would have his gonads.

"To answer your questions, they are going to pay overtime if we get behind schedule. Who says this is going to push us back? We've just gotten started here. And we've only got a few stories on one side to re-frame, so let's start demo on this from the top down. Who's on jackhammers first?"

The team broke for lunch in good spirits. In just a matter of hours, the wall was almost down. The construction site was messy, with big chunks of light gray rock scattered on the ground across from scaffolding that was showing early signs of oxidation. But the demo was almost perfect, with the rest of the walls untouched. They'd have to build back part of the wall they were tearing down, but that was the price of construction. At least it wasn't coming out of his pocket. He just hated that supplies were going to waste. Concrete was not cheap now that everyone wanted a concrete countertop or concrete floors in their homes. Following trends annoyed him.

Though he was satisfied with the project, he was unsure about Fortune meeting his friends. She was right; she'd met most of them in the least ideal way possible. But he and Fortune were together now. It was a different ballgame. Besides, that meeting had been a colossal mistake. This one would be on purpose. He just needed to make sure everyone was on their best behavior. And since most of them were dating—he wasn't sure about Seth—at least everyone had someone to keep them in check.

"Hey, what was it like when your wife—y'know, before she became your wife—met your friends?" Jason asked Austin.

"It was hell." Austin laughed when Jason's eyes widened. "At first. But then, my buddies came around. They saw how I was around her, and they thought I was on my way out."

"Out?"

"Benched. Off the team. Into Married-ville." Austin huffed, the stray hairs in his full gray beard flying outward from his mouth. Austin had been married as long as Jason had known him—at least eight years—but he was only a few years older than Jason. "They were right, of course. But when all of them found their wives, we came back together stronger."

Jason smiled. Things with his friends would turn out fine.

"Well, all of us except Fred. He was a crazy loner, anyway. Who ya seeing now, Reed? Some hot blonde with gigantic tatas?"

Jason raised an eyebrow and gave Austin the side-eye.

Austin put down his sandwich and lifted his hands in surrender. "I'm just saying, man. You've got a type."

"Well, you're right about the tatas." He took out his phone and swiped. A picture of Fortune in a red dress shone on his lock screen.

Austin nodded approvingly. "She's gorgeous. And I'll bet she's a gem to be around."

"She is." Jason's grin grew across his face. He was stupid in love.

"Is it the first time they're meeting her?"

"No. Most of them met her under some, let's say, unfortunate circumstances. No one made a great impression on anyone that night." He took a gulp of water from his water bottle.

"Hmm." Austin picked up his sandwich again and bit into it. He talked around a mouthful of turkey and ham. "Were you naked?"

Jason laughed so hard that water came out of his nose. A few of the day laborers glanced up from their meals. "No!"

"That's a plus. Look, whatever you've got going on with your friends, you can fix it. It's what you do. You fix things. And if this woman is worth marrying, it doesn't matter. If they're true friends, they'll come around."

Austin was right. Jason had always been a fixer. Fixing floor plans, repairing relationships, whatever it was, Jason was sure he could fix it. Arranging this group dinner would be just the thing to fix the awkward negative first impression his friends had of Fortune.

Four

Jason

W HEN HE'D PICKED A date on which Diamond Steak Co. could accommodate the large group, Jason texted the gang. Ranjan responded *I'm in* right away. Graham took a while, but within the hour, he said, *Dani and I are there.* Seth didn't respond to the group. It was a full three days later before Jason got a text from Seth:

> Not going to make it, dude.

The text stung, but Jason wasn't going to change the reservation. Seth would say no until he got a case of FOMO and caved. He'd known Seth would be a sticking point. He was the "Fred" of their group. Seth was most likely ashamed, Jason thought.

When Fortune and Seth first met, they were strangers at a club, and he'd called her a whale, not knowing any of this would happen. He probably thought he'd never see her again. With over a million people in Charlotte, who would have thought he'd insult the one person his friend would fall in love with?

But that was then. Now, Jason loved Fortune, but Seth wasn't even giving her a chance. Jason wasn't going to worry about him. Like Austin's friend, Fred, Seth would eventually come around. Jason could wait it out.

"I'm leaving early on Friday," Jason told Austin. "Big dinner plans." He surveyed the now completed re-blocking of the fourth floor with an approving look. Though the architect's plans for the window additions seemed like overkill, the gigantic holes in the wall allowed a welcoming breeze on the unusually hot January day. He turned to his GC, but the man had his back to him.

Austin was crouched in a corner, examining what appeared to be a random puddle of water. Either the floor sloped, and he was visually calculating how much of a fix was needed, or he was lost in thought. With him, it was hard to tell until he spoke or did something.

Jason continued. "Will you be able to handle the crew for a couple of hours?"

Austin stared for a moment longer, then reared to his full height. "Sure thing, boss. I can get one of the guys in here with some self-leveler and fix this." He turned. "Did you say big dinner plans?"

Jason nodded. "Yeah. The gang's going to meet Fortune."

"That's great. So, this is serious?"

"Yeah." Jason stared out the window holes to the skyline. For the first time since he'd met her, he saw himself marrying her. His friends were gathered around, smiling and happy for him and Fortune at their wedding. Graham would be standing beside him as best man, and Ranjan would be one of his groomsmen. Seth would be in the audience. Or would he? He couldn't see Seth very well. In any case, they would all be happy for him but not as full and happy as he would be when he saw Fortune walking down the aisle in a long, flowing white dress with an extremely tight top. Now he was thinking about Fortune's boobs. *Climb out of the gutter, Reed.* He smiled at his one-track mind. "They're going to love her."

Austin scratched his beard. "Remember what I said about my friends. It may take more than one dinner for them to love her. And some of them may never love her. The important thing is that *you* love her, and they respect that."

Were Austin and Graham sharing a brain? It was like hearing an echo aimed at making Jason worry. But Austin had never met Fortune, and Graham barely knew her. If they had, they would understand his certainty.

"I remember, but I'm not worried. Fortune's going to win them over."

Austin grunted and went back to staring at the puddle.

Jason grinned. If that puddle was the only problem they had, it was going to be a good week.

Jason's phone pinged, indicating a new email message. One of the high schools needed a long-term substitute for their shop teacher. Substituting shop classes was the next best thing to being on a productive job site. It was like a shot of dopamine right to the heart. Between this and most of his friends agreeing to dinner, he felt almost giddy. It had been a while since life doled him a winning hand, but he was glad it was happening now. "I've got to make a call. Be right back."

"Tell that skinny guy on three to come up and bring a level with him," Austin said to the puddle and tilted his head sideways.

"Sure thing, boss." Jason laughed and headed for the stairs.

Later that night, he updated Fortune on dinner plans. He'd come home to her again, or rather he'd stopped by her house after work—when had he started thinking of it as coming home to her?—showered, changed, and settled into her sofa. The grayish-blue dual recliner always made him smile a little as he flashed back to their second kiss, where she'd reclined, and he leaned over her. It had been sweet and full of promise, like her. And like their first group dinner would be.

"Everything is going to go great Friday night. I can feel it."

Fortune crossed from the kitchen to the sofa, bringing drinks, and handed him a bottle of his favorite IPA. Her scrunched eyebrows and pursed full lips conveyed a clear message—yeah, right, you big naïve sucker—as she took a long sip of pink Moscato. But all she said was, "I hope so."

"What do you mean, you hope so?"

"I mean that you're so happy, and I don't want your friends to disappoint you, but what I've seen of them was—"

"Not at their best, trust me." He interrupted. He set both their drinks on the coffee table in front of them and clasped her hands in his. Her palm was cool from cradling the chilled wine. She was still giving him the disbelieving pout, but worry softened the hard edges of her stare. "I've said this before, but it's true, believe me. They're definitely dudes. But they're good dudes."

Fortune sighed and raised an eyebrow. "Seth's a jerk."

"A piece of work ..." he eked out slowly. "And he may not even be there."

That made her pout more. "He doesn't even want to be in the same room with me."

"No, sweetie!" He squeezed her hands. His own were dampening with sweat. He wished for more of that feel-good dopamine from earlier. "I promise it's not you."

She wriggled her hands out of his grasp and reached for her glass. "Oh, I know it's not me." She laughed bitterly, then took a gulp of wine. "But I'm going to be blamed for it."

He shook his head.

She continued as if she hadn't seen him. "I'm going to be me. Every bit of me at this dinner. I don't care who gets ticked off because of it."

He clasped her shoulders and turned her to face him. Wine sloshed in her glass, and her gaze went from the precious pink liquid to his. Frustration crept up his spine, but he wasn't going to let it overcome the positive vibes he'd been feeling all week. Dammit, this was going to work. "No one's going to get ticked off. They're going to love you for you. All of you. Because they'll see what I see in you. You're fun. You're sassy. You're caring." He looked at the glass she still held, and the corners of his mouth kicked up. "You're a lush. You'll fit right in."

He wound his arms around her shoulder blades, pulled her across the sofa console into his embrace, and dissolved their laughter with his kiss.

They kissed and drank and kissed some more on the awkward, cushiony blue sofa. Then they went upstairs and made love, a lazy, slow endeavor that drew his mind from the all-important upcoming dinner and had him dreaming they were on an island beach instead, absorbed only in each other, with the sun warming his naked back and her warmth surrounding his front, no clocks or demanding dude-bros.

But after their session, while Fortune dozed, her right side wedged under him, he couldn't stop hearing Graham's and Austin's almost haunting cautionary messages. He'd be an idiot to think this dinner was going to be a lovefest. Still, they didn't know how wonderful this snoring woman was when she was awake. Hope was still as tangible as her velvet-soft skin and buttery vanilla scent.

When they arrived at Diamond Steak Co., Jason felt the pressure of making sure everyone was comfortable. At least he wasn't worried about the service or the food; his favorite restaurant never failed to treat him like a king, and the steak was mouth-watering.

What did worry him was Seth's arrival—despite him turning down the invite—with Tina, the woman Jason had gone out with right before he met Fortune. She was standing beside Seth at the bar, blood-red shiny lipstick the only makeup she wore, her hair pulled back in a severe sandy blonde ponytail with a bunch of gold pins crisscrossing each other on one side. Both her hands were curled around Seth's bicep, and she was hanging onto every word as he ranted about who knows what with Graham, Dani, Ranjan, and Ranjan's date.

On their first and only date, Jason hadn't been into Tina—despite her obvious hints that she wanted him—and the guys couldn't understand why. Especially Seth. The fact that he'd decided to date Tina himself didn't surprise Jason one bit. But that they were there together, on this of all nights, was enough to raise Jason's blood pressure by at least ten points. What was this guy trying to prove?

"Hon, you okay?" Fortune squeezed his hand and dipped her head to catch his gaze.

He shook his head absently. "Yeah, no. I'm fine," he said, not sure if he really was fine, enraged, or somewhere in between. "Why don't you get to know the ladies while I check on our reservation?" He motioned to where Dani and Tina were breaking off from the bar and headed to the restrooms.

"I'm going to ignore that fifties-era 'go hang with the women' suggestion because I do have to go to the bathroom." She threw him a smirk and a raised eyebrow before following Dani and Tina.

He watched her walk away in her loose-fitting top and her not-quite pants. He wasn't sure if the navy-blue bottoms were real or a dream with their gauzy see-through legs over very short, tight shorts that framed her perfect ass. Fortune wearing those dreamy pants enticed him even more than the restaurant's perfectly seared steak.

"Earth to Reed." Graham waved his hand in front of Jason's face.

"Just appreciating the view."

"I can see that." Graham chuckled and rocked on his heels. "The whole world can see that."

"So, the gang's all here." He faced Graham. "Even the ones who said they weren't coming. And with my former date, no less."

"That's Seth for you."

Jason squinted to keep from rolling his eyes and pouting like a petulant child. At least Seth showed up. "Did you know he was seeing Tina?"

"No idea," Graham said. "You know you keep pouting like that, your face is going to stay that way."

Jason ignored his best friend's attempt at levity. "He's just doing this to get back at me. He said he wasn't coming, and now this?"

"Why does everything always have to be about you?"

"This is my story, right now." Jason jabbed himself in the chest with his index finger. "Get your own crisis."

The two glared at each other for a moment, daring the other to say something. Neither could manage and broke down laughing instead.

Five

Fortune

THE BATHROOMS REFLECTED THE vibe of Diamond Steak Co. Ultra-modern and moody with chrome fixtures, concrete countertops, and dark marble floors. The decor was part of the reason Jason loved it there, but to Fortune, it only amplified the confused, mismatched feeling between the aloof atmosphere and the cheeriness of the staff.

She hoped that mismatch didn't bleed down into the group she was about to meet. She emerged from the stalls at the same time as the other ladies in their party. One was a brunette, the other a blonde.

"I saw you come in with Jason. Are you Fortune?" the brunette asked. She was the tallest of the three, with bone-straight dark brown hair halfway down her back. Her skin was pale, but her full face of impeccably matched makeup was devoid of color. Even her blush was only a shade darker than her skin color.

"Yes. And you are?"

"I'm Dani, Graham's girlfriend. And that's Tina, Seth's date." She pointed to the blonde who was applying another coat of bright red lipstick and not paying them attention. "We're also friends. It's nice to meet you. You look great. Thirty-five?"

"I'm thirty-nine, actually."

"Oh, wow, you look amazing. So, are you divorced?"

A harmless enough question, but it made Fortune feel on edge and guarded. It took her back several months ago when then-potential client Aileen Davenport had asked her the same thing after their meeting. "No, I'm single."

The three exited the bathroom and made their way back to the bar. Dani and Tina looked at each other, passing a glance Fortune couldn't figure out.

"Any crazy baby daddies hanging around?" Tina asked with a tone that sounded a lot like those chicks on *Vanderpump Rules* when they'd had too much to drink. She half-laughed, and her teeth shone blindingly white against her red lips and tanned skin.

Here we go. Were they already starting with the microaggression part of the evening? That hadn't even been subtle; instead, the question felt like a hot poker to the gut.

She plastered a smile that was probably coming across as a grimace, but she couldn't muster the care it took to fix her face. "Those are the worst, right? How crazy is yours?" She gave Tina her best laser-like death stare then turned away from them. "I think we're about to be seated."

She left them and went to Jason's side. Social exhaustion was already creeping in her neck and shoulders, and the dinner hadn't even begun.

"Hey, sweetie, how's it going?" Jason asked, pulling her hand into the crook of his arm and leaning away from his friends to gaze at her.

In any other circumstance, this would have been a loving gesture. But with this crowd and her previous exchange with Dani and Tina, Jason was coming off like a dad about to tell her that she could handle the mean girls and to go back and play. For a moment, she imagined kicking him in the shin like a bad kid. She inhaled deeply. No need to be petty. Of course, she could deal with whatever these two could throw at her, but for one night, she just wished she didn't have to. For one night, she wanted to take off the armor and let someone else fight for her. "It's going okay. I thought I heard that our table was ready."

"Yeah, they are just finding a couple more chairs." He kissed her forehead and smiled. "And good. I knew they'd love you. Almost as much as I do."

Her composure was unraveling on the ends as if Jason had found a stray thread and pulled. She realized she was holding her breath and exhaled, her lips forming the grimace-smile once again. This was going to be the night of the ugly smile.

The other ladies joined their escorts, and the group followed the hostess to their table. Fortune's plan was to steer Jason away from the ladies towards Ranjan and his date, but Jason was a big guy and wasn't easily moved. In the end,

Fortune sat at the circular table with Jason to her right and Dani and Graham to her left. When Tina sat beside Graham, the ladies immediately took out their phones and put them on the table.

Jason cleared his throat and got everyone's attention. "Thanks for coming. Everyone probably knows everyone else by now, but just in case ...." He curled his arm around Fortune's shoulders. "This is my girlfriend, Fortune. Sweetie, this is Ranjan and his date Darren, Seth and his date Tina, and Graham and Dani."

Everyone smiled or waved when they were introduced, except Seth and Tina. Seth chose that moment to signal their waiter, and Tina was buried in her phone, thumbs flying across the screen.

Well, that figures. Fortune leaned across Jason and got Ranjan's attention. "So, Ranjan, how did you get tossed in with this motley crew?"

He smiled at his friends. "College. We were the Eastcoasters."

Dani smiled, her face washed over with a look of nostalgia. She had either heard this story before, or she went to college with them.

"The what? Was that a band?" Tina asked.

Fortune would have laughed at that if it hadn't come from Tina. Except for Seth, the woman gave off the strongest I-dislike-you vibes of the group. Everything she said or did made Fortune want to recoil.

Ranjan laughed and pointed to each of his buddies. "Not with those three all vying to be the front man."

Everyone at the table laughed then. Seth began to protest. "I'm just the ..."

"The keg guy," Jason, Graham, and Ranjan said in unison. The table erupted in laughter.

Ranjan continued while the group settled again. "Because we went to Arizona State, there weren't that many from our side of the country, so we kind of found each other. Graham and Jason were on the golf team together. Sometimes, Student Affairs would room students who were from the East Coast together, too. Jason and I RA'd in the same dorm senior year, and Graham and Seth roomed together most of the time they were there. After college, we all applied for and got jobs in Charlotte because the area was expanding, and we wanted to get back to the East Coast. Plus, Jason's from here; so, here we are."

Graham added, "Who knew I'd still be hanging out with these chuckleheads twenty years later?"

Their waiter interrupted the jovial scene and asked for their orders. Everyone had been to Diamond Steak Co. except Darren, so the others ordered drinks and food, which gave Darren a chance to decide.

After the waiter left, Fortune went back to her Q&A with Ranjan. "And how did you two get together?"

Ranjan and Darren looked at each other and said in sync, "SwipeMatch," and then laughed.

"Wow. Coincidence." Jason and Fortune stared at each other and grinned.

"Wasn't that the app we dared you to go on, Jason?" Seth glanced at Jason and then unrolled his napkin over his appetizer plate. The silverware clanged against it. He glanced at Tina as if he were signaling her for some reason.

She and Dani looked at each other and snickered.

"Emo over there was whining, so we dared him to find someone on this fat chicks' dating app. Funny, neither of you are fat or chicks, Ranjan." Seth's grin was predatory.

"It's an inclusive dating app," Darren said, affronted.

Fortune didn't flinch when she turned Seth's way. "Probably shocked the heck out of you that he found me and fell in love. Almost makes you want to try it, right? But then you've got Tina. You seem perfect for each other."

Jason touched her knee and then grabbed her hand under the table, but she slid free from his grasp.

Ranjan spotted the servers coming into view burdened with trays. "Food's here, thank Krishna."

The group dug into their meals, and for a moment, the awkwardness lifted. Everyone focused on their food, giving a pleasant reprieve from the tense verbal jabs and pointed looks.

Jason whispered, "Good, right?" in Fortune's ear.

She glanced at him and grinned. The gesture felt new on her face, and she realized it was the first time that night she'd smiled without it being forced. She perused the table, still projecting that feeling of positivity and satisfaction, hoping it would be returned. Ranjan and Darren echoed the sentiment back to her. Graham gave her a look of pity, and Dani shrugged and went back to her food. Seth actively ignored her, but Tina outright snarled. Only one word made it to the forefront of Fortune's thoughts: vindictive. What else could she say to make this dinner worse for her and more awkward for everyone else?

Tina put down her fork and leaned forward past Graham and Dani to connect to Fortune's gaze. "You know we used to date. Jason and me."

And there it was.

Jason chewed his bite of steak hurriedly. "One date." He held up an index finger. "It was one date."

"Gosh, this is like an episode of *Friends*," Darren mumbled.

"When have we ever been like *Friends*?" Seth countered.

Dani nudged Fortune. "You know they're talking about the TV show. You know, from the nineties?"

"You mean *Living Single* 2.0? Did you know that show was the blueprint for *Friends*?"

"Well, I ..."

Fortune laughed wryly. Really? Who wouldn't know the show, *Friends*? "Yes, Dani, I've seen it. Who hasn't? Not as funny as *Living Single* but respectable."

"*Living Single* can't be that great. I've never seen it," Tina piped up.

"Just Google it, Tina." Ranjan sighed heavily like he was so tired of her he couldn't muster an explanation. "Or turn on live TV once in a while. It's still in syndication somewhere, for goodness sakes." He glanced at Fortune and threw her a small smile.

Jason chortled.

Fortune elbowed him, and he disguised his outburst as a cough.

Everyone was quiet while they waited for desserts, coffee, or checks. Tension hung in the air above the table like smog on Interstate 77 at rush hour.

Clearly, the dinner wasn't going as great as Jason said it would. In her opinion, this was a disaster.

Six

Jason

THEY WENT BACK TO his place, silent for most of the ride. Jason glanced at Fortune a few times but couldn't discern what she could be thinking or feeling. However, he was proud. His woman had charmed Ranjan and Darren, stood up to Tina and Dani, and ignored Seth's negativity. She was obviously the light of the dinner, and she was his.

"Well, that was painful." Fortune closed the front door behind her and met him at the sofa.

"I thought it was awesome." Jason glanced at her, registered her furrowed brow and snarled upper lip, and corrected himself. "Scratch that. I thought *you* were awesome. The dinner was a tad awkward."

She didn't answer him and stared into nothingness instead. She obviously didn't feel the same.

"Ranjan loved you," he offered.

"That's because he's lovely. But no one else liked me. Some of them actively hated me. Seth, for one." She eased deeper into the sofa—away from him—and crossed her arms. "And one of them was jealous."

He turned to her, confused. "Jealous?"

"Like you didn't notice."

He stared at her with a blank expression.

"Tina?"

She unfolded her arms and shrugged, disbelief slashed across her face. "What's the deal with you and her?"

Oh, crap. A wave of guilt and then defiance went through him. So, what if he'd gone out with her? It was one time. He should have explained this to Fortune before they sat down to dinner, but he'd been blindsided seeing her—with Seth of all people—that he hadn't really thought about Fortune. And there went the guilt again.

"We went out once. One date," he clarified after she sniffed and looked away from him. "Graham set us up after I had been complaining about another failed date. Tina was clingy and vapid, and we just didn't click. In fact, it was after the date with Tina that I went to The Graveyard, and Seth dared me to go on SwipeMatch. Where I found you." He reached over to kiss her, but his lips only caught her cheek.

"Well, however that date went, she doesn't want to see you with anyone that isn't her."

He really didn't want to talk about Tina. She meant nothing to him, and the fact that she was with Seth was disgusting. He didn't want to even think about it. "Her smile is evil.

Her laugh is grating. She's like a snake when it finds a rabbit. That's probably why Seth likes her."

"So, Tina wanted you."

"Past tense. Besides, it doesn't matter because—"

"How can I compete with that?"

Why wouldn't she let this go? He leaned back. "It's not a competition—"

"So, I don't even rate, then?"

"That's not what I—"

She huffed. "Tell me you wouldn't go out with her again if she wasn't with Seth. Tell me it wouldn't be easier to date her instead of me."

He grabbed her arms, hoping to get through to her how much he loved her and how little Tina meant. "I don't want easy! I want you!"

Her eyes widened, and she let out a snarky laugh. "Well, thanks for saying I'm difficult."

"That's not what I meant. You are not listening to me!"

"No! You're the one who's not listening!" She squirmed to get out of his hold. "That woman still wants you. And she did everything she could tonight to make me look like a shrew and turn your friends off me. The last thing I need is my boyfriend's friends calling me an ABW behind my back."

Jason loosened his grasp in confusion. "A what?"

"ABW—Angry Black Woman." Fortune's expression was blank. "Are all your friends prejudiced, or are they just ignorant? It's like they've never socially interacted with a Black person before. I almost wished that someone—any-one—you knew that was Black would show up."

"For one, Tina is with Seth, and two, the fact you're Black has nothing to do with how much they like you. Fortune, they aren't like that. You have to believe me. It was just an off night."

"'An off night'? Are you kidding? Dani was talking to me like I had just emerged from some jungle into civilization, and Tina was challenging me like I was some Sapphire trying to dominate you into being with me."

"What the— A Sapphire?"

"Google it, Jason! I'm not going to explain it to you! I'm tired. Good night." Fortune grabbed her purse and left, slamming the front door.

Jason was stunned as he stared at the door. Why would an awkward dinner with his friends who had been abnormally rude have anything to do with race or Fortune being treated like some type of negative stereotype? They had to figure this out.

Was she going to come back? They needed to talk more about this. He waited for a few minutes, but the door didn't open. Dread churned in his gut. Instead of bringing everyone closer together, this dinner had created rifts where none had been. He trudged up the stairs.

He awoke the next day to an ominous text from Dani:

> Meet me at Free Range in an hour we need to talk.

Jason was sure the dinner hadn't just been awkward. It had been abysmal. The dread from the night before rose up again as he texted his agreement to meet Dani at the fast, casual, earth-friendly deli.

The little bistro was slightly less crowded than on a usual workday when it would be filled with corporate execs and their employees who flooded in from nearby office buildings. His mind flashed back to the last time he was at Free Range: he met Louis and begged for his acceptance and a ticket to his Alzheimer's gala so he could woo Fortune back. Jason was uncomfortable then, and he was uncomfortable now.

When he arrived today, Dani was in line, perusing the overhead menu with a blonde that was partially obscured from his view. The two were chatting in hushed tones, and Jason had the distinct feeling he was walking into an ambush. He'd been set on a chicken club sandwich and one of those gooey sweet confections in their bakery case, but his appetite went out the door as recognition of the blonde set in. Tina. He briefly looked around for not-so-cleverly-hidden cameras or any sign he was on a TV show. A few people stared at the big, tall construction guy as he walked in, with his slightly less-appropriate attire of jeans and a button-down, but that was normal for Jason. Aside from that, everyone was behaving normally.

"Hey, ladies."

The two turned around and gave him pointed but inscrutable looks. Not good. Their stares were sharp, but their faces were blank.

Dani's lips curved up at the ends, the only friendly gesture coming from either of them. "Hey, Jason. Thanks for meeting us."

"Tina. Hope you're having a good day. Wasn't expecting to see you here."

"Did I not mention she was coming? Sorry about that." Dani avoided further discussion by approaching the cashier and ordering.

"Good to see you, too, Jason." Tina's every word had sarcasm dripping from it. She followed her friend to the counter without looking back at him.

That confirmed it. He was screwed.

The three ordered, Dani and Tina getting made-to-order sandwiches, and Jason deciding on an iced matcha green tea instead of the full spread he wanted, and they sat at a high-top close to the door. He'd steered them that way, thinking if he needed to make a quick escape, it would be the most advantageous place.

Tina and Dani sat across the table from him, silent, as they waited for their food. Two pairs of eyes focused on him, and two pairs of arms crossed, practically radiating accusatory vibes. They reminded him of the twins in *The Shining* if one were blonde. He wasn't afraid of them, but if he were honest, he was intimidated by their influence. With one word, Dani could change Graham's mind about anything, and if Graham and Dani were not on board, a dinner redo wasn't going to happen. And from the looks of their faces now and Fortune's storming out the night before, they needed a redo.

Dani started the conversation. "We don't have a choice in who you date, but still. This Fortune chick is a little ..."

"Aggressive, abrasive ..." Tina threw out negative adjectives like they were last week's trash. Her lips were snarled, and her forehead scrunched like a toddler simulating a thinking face.

"Negative. She's got a bad attitude," Dani countered.

Tina pointed at Dani, acknowledging the appropriateness of the word.

"What?" Was he really hearing this right now? Fortune had weathered his friends' inquisition with what he thought was grace and elegance, and they said she had a bad attitude? True, she wasn't her giggling, fun self like when just the two of them would go out, but aggressive and negative? No way.

"I mean, we just asked her if she knew *Friends*. She could have just answered yes or no. We didn't need a TV history lesson or whatever."

"If what she was saying was even true," Dani murmured, barely audible, but he caught the words. And the sentiment.

Tina reached across the table and grasped Jason's free hand. This woman was always touching him. It was annoying. "Listen, you don't need that kind of antagonism in your life. You've got enough stress." She smiled that predatory smile that made him want to get up and run.

Dani chimed in. "She's not going to fit in with the group, Jason. I mean, you could knife the tension at dinner last night. We're all going to be uncomfortable around her."

Jason leaned back, too stunned to speak. Wow, Fortune had been right. They had really called her angry. But to what end? Did Tina really want him back?

This whole scene reminded him of the guy he used to be decades ago—twenty-something and single by choice because relationships always carried too much drama. Women wanted him for no other reason than to be seen with him. Women angry or envious of the woman he was with. "You're one of the good ones," his mom told him then. "Girls recognize that and will try everything to keep one of the good ones."

Now in his forties, he couldn't believe that women would still be that way. Tina and Dani overtly snubbing Fortune was incomprehensible. He didn't even have a clue why Dani was acting like this. She had been with Graham for years. Jason could only surmise that she wanted to support Tina. After all, Dani was the reason he and Tina had gone out in the first place.

"Ladies, you know I respect your opinion. Dani, you're like a sister to me. And Tina—" he pulled his hand from her grasp, "You're with Seth, so you're almost like a friend to me, too. But Fortune is my girlfriend. Whomever I choose to date is none of your business." He wrapped a napkin around his matcha and got up. "Was that what this little meeting was for?"

Tina stared at him, mouth agape.

Dani raised an eyebrow and sipped at her beverage.

Neither spoke.

"Okay. I've got things to do." Namely, apologize to my girlfriend for how my friends treated her last night. "See you later."

Seven

Fortune

AFTER SHE LEFT JASON's place, Fortune headed straight for her best friend Louis's bungalow, needing to sort the night out with someone who hadn't been there and who would be on her side. Louis was great for a vent session, but some of these microaggressions even had him stumped. Not that she was looking to him for advice. But she agreed with his recommendation to see her other BFF, Celeste.

"While I embrace my feminism, I am and will always be a man. This sounds like some of that female cattiness that I don't understand." The two had finished the last season of *Succession* and were yelling at the TV and each other about "privileged white people getting away with blatant crime". For the first time, it struck her as weird—they were making judgments about the imaginary Roy family that Jason's friends made about her. *At least I'm not doing it at the dinner table in front of them.*

With Tina and Jason's history in the picture, though, she knew it wasn't all about race. It was about who they thought was better for him. And Tina seemed at least friend-adjacent. She thought about the famous sitcom again. Tina was Janice—obnoxious and loud but fondly memorable—and Fortune hadn't even been cast.

"You're right. There's definite catty behavior." She flashed back to Jason's bewilderment at the term *ABW* and how oblivious he was about Tina. "And a little ignorance, too."

The next day, Fortune made her way across town to Celeste's house in Ballantyne. Driving through the streets of the south Charlotte neighborhood with densely packed commercial buildings and gated housing developments in pristine condition always made Fortune mutter "new money" as she wound around roundabouts and crept down four-lane roads at the grand speed of thirty-five miles per hour. The neighborhood evolved like it was struggling to find its identity, but it didn't care—high-rise office buildings and hotels on the outskirts of town in the middle of thinning forests, buffered on one side by an interstate, a state line on the other. And more Target shopping centers in a one-mile radius than should even be allowed.

Celeste and her husband were there because they didn't exactly fit in anywhere, either. As progressive as Charlotte was, its neighborhoods remained historically racially divided. While Celeste's net worth would rival half of those in Myers Park, those stately oak trees shaded mostly white faces with old money. And Celeste's husband Mauricio's store was all about high-end luxury items. In fact, the only two truly diverse neighborhoods in Charlotte were the University area and the Mountain Island Lake neighborhood, which was being actively depressed despite the high cost of land and the inflated house prices in the city limits. Maybe Charlotte wasn't as progressive as Fortune had thought.

And maybe her relationship with Jason wasn't as normal as she thought. Even though love was colorblind, society was not. It was too much to ask for everyone to embrace them and accept them as a couple. Screw them if they didn't, though. It was such a Jason thing to say. She chuckled to herself and sighed. She really did love this guy.

Being with him meant she was going to have to put up with his prejudiced friends. But it didn't mean she would stop being herself or trying to educate them along the way.

Fortune pulled into Celeste's driveway and texted her arrival, then gazed up at the two-story transitional Mc-Mansion painted in alabaster and trimmed in charcoal gray. The shutters, the door, and even the gutters had been custom-painted in gray to match. She called it the "Real Housewives of Charlotte" house, or RHOC house for short. And Celeste was classier and more flamboyant than all the other housewives combined.

She came sweeping out of the front door like a lady who lunched, with a thin beige and orange caftan covering a blouse, navy wide-legged pants, and designer shoes. The outfit had to have been custom made because you couldn't find anything that flattering or stylish in a department store for a plus-size woman nearly six feet tall. Owning a thriving design studio had its perks.

Celeste perched a hand on her hip as if she were auditioning for said featured housewife. "Are you coming in or what?"

"You know I always have to marvel at Black excellence." She got out and followed Celeste inside.

"It's a house. I mean, we all have to live, right?"

"Yeah. But there's living, and then there's this." Fortune gestured to the impeccably clean, simply gorgeous space around and in front of her—a grand foyer with porcelain-tiled entry. To her left, French doors closed off Celeste's home office, done in pastels like a French boudoir. Her husband's smaller office to the right resembled a men's lounge more than an office, with leather seating and a dry bar in the back. They'd had the home custom-built with offices in the front for easy client entry and exit. A powder room was tucked beside Celeste's office for that same reason. In front of them was the open-concept living room, dining room, and kitchen with a massive marble-topped island. The decor was neutrals everywhere except for the gold fixtures and cabinet hardware and the green and blue accessories here and there—Mauricio and Celeste's favorite colors.

The island was laden with the most massive charcuterie board Fortune had ever seen. Celeste had these boards laden with all her favorites—cheese, olives, honey, jam, all types of crackers and bread including Fortune's favorite roti bread, fruit, dips, sushi, shrimp, deli meats, petit fours, and brownies. It was more like a smorgasbord than a charcuterie board.

"You brought out the big guns. This must be serious."

Celeste poured sparkling water for them. "You tell me. You called at like one-thirty in the morning."

"To be fair, I had stopped by Louis's place, and we got caught up in one of our binge-watch sessions."

"What happened last night?"

Fortune relayed the events of the night from the awkward dinner to the heated discussion with Jason afterwards. Her best friend listened with a captivated stare while she munched on squares of various yellow and white cheeses. The pair had met in college, and while they also had a friend group—five of them, compared to Jason's foursome—Fortune was closer to Celeste than the others, mostly because of the many conversations they had like this, with Celeste listening intently while Fortune spilled her guts, then offering sage advice because she was a whopping four months older than Fortune and, therefore, decades wiser.

"I'm probably asking too much of these people." Fortune sipped the sparkling water and coughed. The pear flavor twanged on her tongue, and the bubbles tickled her nose. "He's like George Clooney was in the two-thousands—an eligible, good-looking guy who has a couple of coins to rub together and has managed to stay single and childless for forty years. You don't expect George Clooney to end up with a fat Black woman from Nebraska."

"Are there even Black people in Nebraska?"

"You know, Malcolm X was from there."

"I know, but still ... Nebraska? The only thing whiter is Iowa. Or maybe Denmark." Celeste laughed.

"See, we can laugh about this because we know it's an ignorant thing to say. They would either legitimately ask or would weaponize it."

Celeste inhaled sharp and noisy. "Wow. Tough crowd."

"Yeah. And these are the closest people to Jason outside of his family." There was always a caveat to every relationship she'd been in. She'd thought her crush on Graham and the one disastrous date would be the only hiccup, but no such luck.

"In any case, it doesn't matter who they think or expect him to date. They should respect whoever he *is* dating."

"It's really this Seth guy. They all call him a jackass like he's that way with everyone. But I'm pretty sure he's a racist, not just a garden-variety jerk with no filter."

"Great." A look of solace crossed Celeste's face.

"What's wrong with him? Doesn't he know it's the twenty-first century?" Fortune repeatedly balled her hands into fists.

"And no one is racist in the twenty-first century?" Celeste countered. "Where have you been? Living under a rock in a rainforest somewhere?"

"I mean, why do I have to be in a rainforest? It's because my hair is frizzy, isn't it?" Fortune fluffed her curls and then smoothed them over.

The two guffawed.

She loved hanging out with Celeste and wished they did this more often. It was like being back in college again—minus the crying girls and the scent of cheap beer in dorm hallways—being able to laugh at your troubles and put them away, at least during the time they hung out together. And, unlike her friendship with Louis, there was something more authentic between them. Maybe it was because they'd literally grown into adulthood in college, each understanding the pains of menstrual cramps and broken hearts and supporting each other through both.

Right now, it was probably because, at some point, they'd endured the sting when they'd been reminded via various relationships how society viewed Black women. They'd been passed up for white girls, treated like backup choices, and generally neglected. Celeste had found her soulmate, and Fortune thought she had steeled herself against these "spirit attacks" (as she called them) over the years—this negative treatment just because her skin was darker than two-thirds of the country's population.

But she realized as she sipped her water that she had cracks in her spirit armor. She had been wounded last night, tiny microaggressions and disgusted looks chipping away at her soul. And the attack hadn't stopped at the dinner. Jason had wounded her, too, with how he'd overlooked anything racial and explained away Tina's behavior. As if Fortune had to accept the woman was competition, even if Tina had no chance at winning the game of get-the-guy.

"How am I going to deal with this? I can't take him away from his friends."

"Sometimes, white folks need a minute to turn their fear alarms off and turn on their 'oh, you're an actual human, not just a stereotype' alerts."

"You're silly. But yeah, I get it. Endure a few more dinners."

Celeste headed to the kitchen for more sparkling water. "And invite us to the next one, please? I've gotta witness this train wreck."

"So now, it's a train wreck."

"I'm just saying!"

But Celeste was onto something. If Fortune brought her friends to the inevitable dinner redo, this severely insular group could get some exposure to different people ... and maybe some understanding.

Eight

Jason

FOR THE NEXT COUPLE of weeks, Jason absorbed what Fortune, Dani, and Tina had said. He still owed Fortune an apology because the other ladies had indeed been so negative about Fortune. And he had to admit, Tina was probably jealous, and Dani could have been in league with her. After all, they were friends. Both could have wanted Tina to end up with him.

But he didn't think their negativity had anything to do with Fortune being Black. His friends weren't racist. And even though he didn't know Tina all that well, he did know Graham and Dani would never set him up with someone who was that far from his mindset. At least Dani wouldn't. They didn't want him with Fortune because she wasn't the one they had chosen for him. In effect, Tina was. His friends obviously wanted to see him happy if they had gone through this much trouble, but for some reason, they couldn't see how happy he was with Fortune.

Jason walked into the neighborhood high school shop classroom just before the students swarmed in. Today was a welcome break from the chaotic job site that was now half-covered in rubble from last week's remodel. When he substituted for a shop teacher, he looked forward to sharing his expertise and enthusiasm for his work. His favorite times were when he got to sit in on students completing wood-working projects, bringing back his love of carpentry and making art out of blocks of wood.

Jason sat on the edge of the teacher's desk at the front of the room and watched as the now-familiar group of students took their seats. The full-time shop teacher had taken parental leave almost a month ago after his wife gave birth to their first child, so he'd seen these students once a week for the past few weeks.

"Okay, class, we're going to give our projects a final editing and polishing in the next two weeks. If you're already finished with your project, I will give you the next assignment so you can create a build plan that can be executed safely."

"Hi, Mister Reed," said a tall young woman with long, bone-straight hair as she walked in. Trailing behind her was a boy with thick glasses and blond hair that was shoulder length and shaggy on the ends.

"Nice of you to join us, Ashley. Sam."

"Hi, Mister Reed." Sam hurried to the counter-height table that he shared with Ashley.

"Okay, so as I said, we're finishing up our creations. But don't forget the after-project analysis Mister Taylor asked you to complete. Make sure you fully answer all four discussion questions and upload the assignment to the course site. I'll be coming around to see if you have questions."

Most of the students went to the back of the room to pick up tools and supplies for the projects they had been working on. Each student had their own project, but they shared tools because there weren't enough to go around. In public schools that still had technical education classes, there were never enough tools to go around. And now that Mr. Taylor had his own kid, he wasn't likely going to delve into his own pocket anymore.

It was such a disconnect. As a construction manager in a growing city, he could never find enough skilled tradesmen to help complete all the work up for bid. He had to turn down more than a few jobs just because he didn't have the personnel. And here he was with the next generation of potential tradesmen, unable to train them for a lucrative and rewarding career because blue-collar workers weren't valued. His father's face ran through his thoughts, followed by an idea. Jason should start a program where construction companies donated used tools to public school technical programs, thus shining a light on the disconnect between what society wanted you to grow up to be and what it actually needed to function.

Jason took out his phone to text Fortune and see what she thought. Her face was staring back at him from the lock screen, and he remembered they were at an impasse, barely checking in with each other since the dinner. He hadn't seen her, talked to her, or researched any of those terms she'd said. They'd pressed pause on their relationship without even knowing it.

"Mister Reed, this isn't coming out smooth."

"Sam, that's because you're sanding against the grain." Jason jammed his phone in his pants pocket, adjusted his safety glasses, and guided Sam on the right way to sand wood.

After Sam made a few passes, Jason was satisfied enough that he could move on. He circuited the room a few more times, helping where needed and giving accolades for good work done.

While Jason mentored, he overheard Ashley and Sam chattering under their breaths to each other as they huddled over their projects. "I saw the lock screen on his phone! It's a woman in a red dress, and I don't think she's famous. That's gotta be his girlfriend!"

"Whatever you say, Ashley."

"And she's Black!" Ashley nudged Sam, and he stopped sanding and faced her. "Sam, he likes Black girls! I've got a chance."

Sam sighed heavily. "He's also our sub. Get it? He's a teacher. He's old."

He was the hot teacher. But, old? Wow, that hurt. Jason smiled despite himself. He walked the aisle beside Sam and Ashley's workstation, pretending he hadn't heard them, and dug his phone out of his pocket.

Fortune's eyes twinkled, and her smile warmed his heart every time he looked at the lock screen photo. He'd snapped it after she had gotten dressed the morning after the gala, despite Fortune not wanting him to. Her face was devoid of makeup, her dress was wrinkled, and her lips were puffy from all the kissing they'd done moments before. She was extraordinary.

But until Ashley had said it, he hadn't even thought of Fortune as a "Black girl". He wasn't stupid; he knew she was Black, but he didn't see her that way. He saw Fortune, a woman who happened to be Black. But that wasn't the way other people saw her.

He replayed what Dani and Tina had said, only this time, he heard it with Fortune's race filter. Even his friends saw her ethnicity first and formed opinions before they'd gotten to know her. Maybe they'd even justified their own backward thinking with her defensive responses. *She doesn't fit in with the group. We're going to be uncomfortable* .... It was ignorant.

Then again, not even recognizing her ethnicity at all was probably just as ignorant.

Sam cleared his throat. "Mister Reed, it's fifteen 'til two."

Jason snapped out of his thoughts, glanced at the plastic clock on the wall, confirmed the time on his phone (in case some bright kids had messed with the clock), and turned to the teenagers. "Okay, class. Let's put away our supplies. If you're finished with your projects, put them on the back shelf to be graded. If you're not, put them on the side shelf for next time." He perched on the edge of the desk, worried about what he'd exposed Fortune to at that dinner.

Ashley's not-so-quiet whisper to Sam drifted over the other students' banging and rustling. "He was really looking at his phone. Do you think he heard us?"

After the teenagers emptied the class, Jason searched the Internet for ABW sapphire. Links referred to the term as a racist stereotype, a caricature of a loud, rude, obnoxious Black woman. The phrase "sistas with attitude" was repeated. There was even a twenty-something page essay by a Dr. Carolyn West, PhD about the term and other disparaging phrases directed at assertive Black women.

But what struck him most were the images. Cartoons from the early 1900s showing rotund women with dark skin and exaggerated lips running after skinny cowardly men to 1970s movie posters for *Foxy Brown* and *Coffy*, showing highly sexualized females toting firearms, even that *New Yorker* cartoon cover showing First Lady Michelle Obama in the Oval Office holding a machine gun and strapped with bullets. None of these were how he saw Fortune. But what if the rest of the world saw her like this? Saw all Black women who spoke their minds like that? What if this was how Dani and Tina had seen her?

He blanched, a burst of guilt hurtling through him, then leaned an elbow on his desk and clamped a hand over his eyes. Words and phrases Tina and Dani had said floated back to his memory. Aggressive, abrasive. *Attitude.* Fortune was right. It wasn't just jealousy. There was racial prejudice there, too, and he'd missed it.

Before he could perform any more searches or think of ways to fix the situation, his phone vibrated along the desk and bumped his elbow. The alarm he'd set to remind him to head back to work brought him back to the present. He'd have to figure this out later.

Nine

Jason

H E RODE BACK TO the work site then all the way home preoccupied with what Fortune could have been going through after the dinner. Other than the brief talk about ABWs, she'd given no inkling she was upset or worried about being the only Black person at the dinner, how his friends would interact with her, or even how they would perceive her. He'd thought she was just apprehensive because she'd met them under not-so-good terms.

If the situation were reversed, Jason would have been a wreck. Though he wouldn't admit it if asked, he was often bothered when people were less than comfortable around him. He noticed when people shirked from the tall guy in the dirty boots whenever he walked into a lunch spot, and it put him on alert. She was probably well set on how people saw her—as Black and female first—and was prepared for whatever they would throw at her. Jason couldn't understand how you could get used to that. How did someone go through life like that?

On the other side, how could his friends not see Fortune despite their prejudice? Surely, he wasn't the only one who saw beauty outside his race? No, he wasn't. Graham had dated a bunch of women from different races. But they all looked like Dani—slim, long, straight dark hair, plain or no makeup, no curves. Seth had never dated outside his race, opting to date women that were essentially a version of Tina—blonde, thin, and made up like a YouTube make-up tutorial. Ranjan had never dated an Indian guy, which could have been defiance against his parents, but still, most of his boyfriends had been white. In fact, Darren had been the first Black guy he'd ever seen Ranjan with, and Jason had met him at the dinner.

Fortune was right; they didn't know how to act around her because none of them had ever really been friends with a Black woman. And they thought they were progressive enough having a gay Indian guy in the group. Not that they had ever consciously thought about it in that way; Ranjan was always just their buddy. Now that Jason had analyzed it, he had felt a certain social superiority when Ranjan was around. Like he was woke or whatever people said. Thinking the word was like slime inside his skull. Ugh. Being woke was starting to feel a lot like being pretentious and ignorant at the same time.

However, they seemed to be at a stand-off—his friends on one side, Fortune on the other, and him in the middle. And he couldn't figure out how to fix that.

But he did need to apologize to Fortune. Plus, he wanted to see her so badly his body throbbed from their lack of closeness. He grabbed his phone and headed out the door, sure that she would be home and let him in.

When Jason got to Fortune's house, she was in the kitchen, pulling a cheesecake out of the oven. Well, that was unexpected. It was just a regular old Tuesday. A Tuesday with cheesecake, apparently.

"I'm trying a new recipe. Cinnamon pecan caramel. It's supposed to taste like a cinnamon roll inside of a cheese-cake." She sat the springform pan on a trivet to cool.

"Smells delicious. What brought this on?"

"Not sure." She turned her back to him and poked in the refrigerator. "I really need a wine fridge."

"Fortune," Jason sing-songed. He took her in his arms, pushing the fridge door closed so she would let go of it. "Don't avoid the question. As much as I love cheesecake, this isn't your normal MO. Why are you cooking cheesecake on a school night?"

She threw him the most vicious side-eye, as if to say they would've never hung out if they'd gone to any of the same schools. Then she sighed, and the viciousness faded out of her stare. In his arms, her body slumped.

An immediate need to support her shot through him, and he clutched her tighter.

"After the dinner, I was annoyed and irritated. I tried to get along with your friends, but they're so ..."

He sighed heavily. "Unlikeable?"

"Oblivious. Do they think before they talk? Regardless, I shouldn't have taken that out on you." She turned out of his grasp and released the cheesecake from its springform. "So, I thought I'd bake you an apology cheesecake. I'm sorry for the way I acted."

He spotted the layer of pecans and brown sugar and wondered if this was a bit of what Heaven must be like on Tuesday. A nutty, syrupy aroma swirled around him and made him dizzy with craving. He could almost feel the velvety texture of the cream cheese on his tongue. This would be one of the best cheesecakes he'd ever had.

Wait a minute. *She* was apologizing to *him?* Well, that was backward. His student Ashley's comments floated back into his mind. "I was just thinking—"

"Thinking that your friends don't want me around. Yeah, I know."

Jason shook his head. "No. I was thinking about how hard it must be for you to live in a world where people see your color and judge you before they get to know you. My friends didn't make it easier. I'm the one who should apologize. I'm sorry for having you sit through that."

Fortune looked up from her cheesecake preparations, and the corners of her lips lifted. "Thanks. If you saw that, maybe the others will see it too. Surely, I can stomach another dinner with them and find out. Maybe I can bring my friends next time. Take the pressure off."

When she peered into his eyes, he had to force himself not to kiss her. They were being contrite and trying to solve social problems, so he had to stay focused. But the smell of sugar combined with thoughts of eating cheesecake off her naked body made it hard to concentrate on serious conversation.

"We should hang out instead of having another dinner. Do something more fun," Jason blurted as he shook off dreams of sugar and sex. "So, they can really get to know you, and let go of their hangups." The idea just came to him, but it made sense. He went back to his friends' parochial social experience, how the woman they saw for him probably looked nothing like Fortune. But it was because they didn't know Fortune. If they knew her, they would all come around. The answer was to give them more chances to hang out with her and fall in love.

She was quiet for about a minute looking past him instead of at him. He couldn't figure out the look on her face; it was introspective, but that was it. What was she feeling? Was she humiliated by the idea? Did she think it was silly?

But then she said something surprising, and he fell in love with her all over again. "Let's do karaoke."

The Graveyard was packed with college basketball fans, rabid for local divisional championships that set up March Madness brackets. The Eastcoasters' favorite bar never really resembled its namesake, always bustling with energy and alive with people's conversations bouncing off the cavernous loft ceiling. Its exterior at the end of a mini strip mall in the parking lot of a bigger strip mall was so unassuming that newcomers always looked shocked when they opened the door to a packed room that sounded like a stadium.

The whole neighborhood seemed to be there. Ranjan had even brought Darren, but he left before Seth dragged in a full twenty minutes after the group's decided-upon time to meet. Jason hadn't been to their favorite bar with the guys since the night he'd fought with Seth in the parking lot. His behavior that night—and since—was why they were in this situation now.

Jason took a swig of his IPA. "Guys, I think we should get to know each other's partners."

The group all spoke at once.

"Get to know in what way exactly?" Ranjan asked.

"I don't swing, especially not with any of you," Seth said.

"I knew you had a thing for Dani!" Graham shouted.

The guys looked at Graham.

Jason rubbed his forehead and sighed, coaxing his eyebrows down from meeting his hairline. He didn't expect he'd have to explain and persuade. They'd known each other for so long they could probably read each other's minds if they tried hard enough. Though maybe it was best that they hadn't. "No one wants Dani except you. Man, your ego is big." He took another gulp of beer. "What I meant was we should go on group dates. The dinner was ..." He waved his hand over the table in a seesaw motion. "Well, it could have gone better. But we got over that awkwardness, and now we can really get to know everyone. Maybe even have some fun together."

"Group dates?" Graham asked.

"Group dates," Jason confirmed.

Ranjan laughed. "You heteros. This is not an ABC ensemble drama! This is real life. And if that dinner proves anything, it's that we don't all get along. Well, except for Fortune and me. She's delightful."

Seth piped up. "That's what this is about. Us getting along with your girlfriend." He poked Jason in the chest. "I don't need to waste my time getting to know her. I know enough. She's trouble."

Jason set down his beer and grabbed Seth's hand, squeezing it in his grip and watching him grimace. "Get this straight. I love Fortune. She's here to stay. So, if you want to hang out with us, you'll be nicer to her. Got it?"

Seth's response was strained. "Yeah, man. Got it."

Jason let go of Seth's hand and picked up his beer again, gulping it and feigning nonchalance. This group date idea could be a problem, but he wasn't going to explore that now. "So, how about karaoke next Friday?"

Ten

Fortune

"I SHOULDN'T HAVE TO twist your arm about this," Fortune sang into the dashboard of her car. She was headed home from a day at the illustrious Davies Marketing. She laughed internally at the sarcastic tone of the thought. Even though she loved her job as a seminar creator, when talking with a woman who owned a million-dollar company, everything she did seemed like small potatoes. Even when said woman was your best friend.

"I thought you said it would be a dinner redo. Not a session of let's make complete fools of ourselves." A barrage of barking came through the car's speaker, followed by Celeste's shushing.

"You said you wanted to see a train wreck. This is sure to be one for the ages."

"I wanted to see one, not be in the middle of one. Sit, Cheeto!" Celeste must have just come in and was being greeted by her hungry dogs, Cheeto and Sunshine, twin doodles. Every day they could, she and Mauricio would get together for lunch and trade wins or horror stories that'd happened that morning. It was the best time of her day, Celeste often said. Fortune thought it was probably because it was a brief moment away from the stress of managing a business while spending that time with the one you loved.

When Jason started coming over after work, she felt that same comfortable peace. It was a welcome intimacy she'd never had with a boyfriend before. She wondered if Jason felt it, too.

Fortune snapped out of her musings. "I'm pretty sure it won't be a train wreck. And if it is, hey! We'll be laughing at ourselves too much to be horrified about it. And did I mention it's at that bar in NoDa? The one with the tower of bottles in the center?"

"Using the promise of lots of alcohol to sway me. Okay, Edwards. I'm in."

Fortune rode with Louis and Celeste to the bar just north of Uptown Charlotte to NoDa, the artsy community, and the neighborhood with the best vegan restaurant. Jason was coming straight from his office and a quick stop by the job site to make sure everyone had left for the night. He would drop Fortune off later while Celeste's husband would pick her up after his dinner with clients.

It was a lot of coming and going, like group outings in college when the logistics of too many people and too few cars made getting from one place to another interesting.

Fortune shuddered as she remembered how most of those college outings ended up in drama and tears, and once stranded in the living room of some strange guy's house with the guy's roommate silently staring at her like a psychopath while a friend and the strange guy did who knows what upstairs. Well, everyone knew what. Fortune was only glad for soundproof floors. Tonight, what she most wanted was for everyone to go home happy.

As Louis parked, Darren and Ranjan got out of a car one row in front of them. Fortune hopped out and smiled, happy to see her favorite couple of the group. "Hey, y'all. Ranjan and his boyfriend are here. I love them!" she said to her friends before dashing over to meet the couple.

Ranjan embraced her in a warm hug. He smelled like sandalwood and peppermint, and she was having a hard time letting him go. "My dearest Fortune," he said, his British accent heavier than usual. "I love seeing you again, but you've got to tell me."

"Yes?"

"Was this your idea? Because as fun as Jason is, I don't see him coming up with this."

"Well, he did come up with fun." She grinned sheepishly. "But yeah, this was the first thing that popped into my head."

"You know? This just might be fun. Even if it's a train wreck." They laughed as the other friends gathered.

"Celeste said almost the same thing!" She turned and pointed to her plus ones. "Celeste and Louis, I'd like you to meet Jason's college buddies Ranjan, Graham, and Seth, and their dates Darren, Dani, and Tina. Folks, these are my besties, Celeste and Louis."

Everyone circulated the group, shaking hands and reintroducing themselves. Tina and Seth were surprisingly civil, but Louis and Darren wouldn't shake hands, opting only to nod to each other.

"What's going on with you two?" Fortune whispered to Louis as they headed for the karaoke bar.

"What do you mean?"

"I know you're not going to play innocent. You just snubbed Darren!"

Louis gave her the death stare. "I did not snub him. But I'm also not going to go up and hug a guy I used to date when he's with someone else."

"What? When did this happen? And more importantly, why didn't I know this?"

"Because there's nothing to tell."

"But—"

"But nothing, girlie." Louis shushed her as they walked inside the bar behind everyone else. "This is not the time to tell that story." He ushered her in, pushing her to join the group. "Aren't you our host until Jason shows up?"

The venue was a true bar with dim blue lighting, stools for seating, and so much alcohol, even passersby could smell it in the air outside the bar's open front door. The space was fashioned as a big shotgun hallway, lined on both sides with booths, and in the middle, a huge circular bar with seating all around it. Directly opposite the entrance, at the back wall was a spotlight stage with two small screens facing the stage and one huge screen behind the stage facing the room. Off to the left of the stage, a DJ booth was tucked into a corner and surrounded by small tables of thick black three-ring binders.

Fortune acted as host all of ten seconds before Jason sauntered in, doling out heys and high-fives like he was the local NFL team's star quarterback meeting fans after a winning game. He gave Fortune a quick peck on the lips before joining Graham to catch up on whatever the news was and presumably to give her time with her own friends.

Everyone settled into the booth lining the right wall of the space nearest the stage. Seated at the bar in front of them were a group of women in their twenties cheering a bride-to-be while she downed a flight of tequila. Fortune hoped Celeste would never ask her to do that if Fortune ever got engaged. "No bachelorette parties," she whispered to Celeste.

"You keep saying that, and I'm going to keep ignoring you. I'm getting you back for mine. That's that."

Fortune hid her grin behind her hand as she thought back to the stripping party bus they had rented for Celeste's bachelorette. Most of the women were in their thirties, but they were acting like rowdy drunk teenagers that night. All except Celeste, who was thoroughly annoyed but played along.

But now that she was almost forty with no proposals in her past or her future, she probably wouldn't need to request it anymore. She'd fallen hard for Jason, but if his friends hated her, how far could this really go?

"Who's singing first?" Dani asked. She had left her table and was heading back with a large black binder in her hands, the logo of the karaoke company on the front.

Graham piped up. "Let's make it a competition. Whoever gets the most applause wins."

"I'll be the judge." Jason raised his hand.

"Um, no. Biased."

Ranjan and Darren volunteered. "We'll do it."

"I'm okay with that," Dani said.

Everyone nodded.

"Boys against girls?" Graham asked.

"Nah," Seth said. "I'm going with Fortune and Celeste."

A lull floated over the group at his statement.

Celeste leaned into Fortune to keep the rest from hearing. "I thought you said he was the one who hated fat Black chicks? Why's he picking us?"

Fortune asked aloud, "Why us? I mean, it's us. That's obvious, but still. Why?"

"I want to win. And everyone knows Bla—*African-American* women of a certain size can sing. Aretha Franklin, Jennifer Hudson." Seth stood a little taller and smirked.

She wanted to punch him in the face.

The rest of the group was silent—Graham looked at his shoes, Tina, Dani, and Darren were wide-eyed, and Ranjan and Jason had annoyed-looking, scrunched faces. Louis and Celeste were shooting daggers from their eyes.

Fortune instead took a more pensive approach. "Hmm. Okay, I see where you're coming from. You're wrong about that, though. First, Jennifer Hudson's lost a lot of weight, and she still sounds great. Second, Aretha Franklin was not plus size when she started her career, and her second and third albums are collectors' items. And lastly, let's demonstrate how we sound. Louis, want to join us?"

Louis nodded and smiled. "Let's go."

Inside, Fortune's insides were churning with excitement and irritation. She loved a good karaoke session because she loved to sing. She could even carry a tune, or so she thought. Well at least there were never any complaints when she sang in public. But now that Seth brought up this stereotype, a good time at a karaoke bar turned into showing up a racist jerk instead. Still, she was determined to have fun doing it.

They picked a fun oldie-but-goody, "Lady Marmalade" by Patti LaBelle and the Bluebells. It was one you had to have chops to sing, but even if you didn't, you could still have fun doing it. The announcer called for "BBBWs and a Skinny Dude" and Fortune, Louis, and Celeste walked up, laughing and trading knowing glances.

Celeste whispered to Fortune. "What are you thinking?"

"Sound as bad as possible," Fortune responded. She nudged her bestie, turned to the audience, and pasted on a fake smile. "Hey all, we're a couple of big, beautiful Black women and a skinny dude here to perform for y'all." She glanced at Seth as the introductory music began to play. "And prove a point while we're doing it."

The trio sang as loudly and as awful as they possibly could. By the end, it sounded like three cats had been rounded up in a bag and tossed in a car's trunk. Despite the sound, Fortune and her best friends put on a show that could rival

Jennifer Lopez's show in Vegas. Celeste and Fortune sandwiched Louis in a suggestive dance during the first chorus. Fortune hip-checked both of them during the second verse and took center stage. Then, at the break, she gyrated behind a bent-over Louis. The performance ended with Louis doing a full split in front of the ladies.

The song garnered a thunderous applause.

"Still think 'African-American women of a certain size can sing'?" Fortune asked Seth.

Seth stuck a finger in his ear. "Obviously, not all of them. I think I've got hearing damage."

"That was the best!" Ranjan hugged a stunned Fortune. "Who's got to follow that up?"

A few other patrons took the stage after BBBWs and a Skinny Dude, and the crowd calmed a bit. Then Dani and Graham did a duet of "Islands in the Stream" and garnered respectable cheers.

Then Seth and Tina were called up. Tina grabbed Dani's arm as she walked past and dragged her back on stage. The intro beat to "Baby Got Back" by Sir Mixx-a-Lot reverberated through the room.

Fortune, Louis, and Celeste exchanged glances.

As soon as Dani realized the song and that she was to play one of the snobby racist white girls in the introduction, she shook her head and walked offstage, forcing Tina to do both parts of the introductory dialogue herself. Seth rapped with flailing arms and random off-beat movements all over the stage. Tina tried to keep up as a makeshift backup dancer, but he largely ignored her and even bumped into her a few times. At the line referring to small waists in relation to big butts, Seth grabbed Tina around the waist, emphasizing how small she really was. Unfortunately, she didn't have the Sir Mixx-a-Lot size-approved backside to match, so the demonstration fell short of its goal, which Fortune was certain was to disparage her size.

This was going to get old very fast. Fortune wondered if Jason's friends were going to tolerate Seth's antics or call him out on them at some point. One thing was certain: if Seth didn't change his behavior, these group dates Jason had put so much hope on were going to become a nightmare.

Eleven

Jason

THE WHOLE WAY HOME, Jason thought about that first song Fortune and her friends sang. They all were out of tune, each of them seeming tone-deaf as they muddled through what he thought was a pretty hard song. Their subsequent selections were no better. Her duet with Louis was so off-key that it could break glass.

Something was off about that. He'd heard Fortune sing before in the shower. While everyone sounded better in the shower, she sounded terrific. She could at least carry a tune.

He parked in her driveway and followed her inside even though he'd told himself he was just going to drop her off. The curiosity about the singing was eating at him.

"Hey, what happened to the singing tonight? Did Louis and Celeste throw you off or something? Because they couldn't carry a tune in a bucket."

"I'm not much better."

He bent his head to look her in the eye. "Um, sweetie, yes you are. I've heard you sing before."

"Yelling at the top of my lungs at the peak of sexual pleasure is not singing, Kemosabe."

"No." He failed at suppressing a grin. "I don't mean that. I've heard you sing in the shower and hum along to the radio. You're good."

Fortune sighed. "Okay. I can sing. But that's the stereotype, isn't it? The big Black girl who can sing. The big woman with the pipes. I didn't want to play into that tonight. Did you see what Seth did? Did you hear what he said?"

Jason grasped her shoulders. "Don't play into that fool. He must be going through something and projecting his bad attitude on other people. I've seen him do this before. I don't know why he's doing it now, though."

"He's doing it to certain people. Me, Celeste, Louis. He even gave Ranjan a look tonight. And that man is utterly delightful." She said the last two words in a poor copy of Ranjan's British accent.

Jason smiled, stepping to close the gap between them. "You've got to admit, though. Other than Seth, tonight was kind of fun. I think they're starting to come around."

She paused for a moment. "Yeah, tonight was actually kind of fun. But let's not get ahead of ourselves here. Seth is like one-fourth of your best-friend group."

"I wouldn't call him a *best* friend, exactly. He's just ..."

"The keg guy. I know. That's getting old. Mainly because you're all too old to be throwing keggers, but still." Her deadpan look made it hard for Jason not to laugh.

"Anyway, I believe it's going to work. A few more group dates will fix all the damage that dinner did." He gave her a quick peck on the forehead and wrapped his arms around her in a hug. "They'll be falling in love with you before you know it."

Twelve

Fortune

FORTUNE GUESSED IT WAS fitting to have a second group date at an adult arcade, since her second date with Jason was there. It had been a fun night, and recreating that would be no small feat, but if anyone could do it, her boyfriend could.

The arcade was in Uptown in the entertainment district, collectively known as the Epicenter even though only one building was named that. They met on the street level of the center's parking garage near the elevator. Most of Jason's friends showed up at the same time as them, but with Louis opting out-claiming that he had another engagement—and Celeste and her husband running a little late, the small talk was more than a little strained.

When Celeste and Mauricio showed up, Fortune almost bowled her best friend over in a hug. "Get me out of here," she whispered frantically to Celeste but let out a small chuckle.

"Is it that bad already?" Celeste whispered back.

"No, I'm bugging."

Jason held her elbow. "Are you going to let Celeste up for air?"

Fortune backed away enough for Jason to give Celeste a hearty hug. "How ya doing, Celeste?"

She laughed. "I'll be doing even better once I kick everyone's butt in some Ms. Pacman."

"Oh, you're on," Graham challenged.

"I thought that was your game, sweetie?" Jason clasped Fortune's hand.

"Stop trying to get a rivalry going between friends!" She planted a kiss on his cheek.

"Everyone, this is Celeste's husband, Mauricio Parisi." Fortune pointed to and introduced members of the group. "This is Jason, Dani and Graham, Darren and Ranjan, and Seth and Tina."

"Ciao, signore e signori," he greeted everyone. He double-kissed the ladies, starting with Fortune, but wisely opted to shake the guys' hands.

Seth looked at Mauricio with a confused glare as they shook hands. "You're Italian?"

"Si." Mauricio's smile was more like a grimace.

Fortune empathized. She couldn't count how many times white people had questioned her when she didn't fit into their box of what a Black person was. She had a Master's degree? Wow, what an accomplishment! She was from Nebraska? Wow, didn't know Black people lived in Nebraska.

Of course, it would be Seth asking the stupid questions tonight. "Wow, I didn't know Black people lived in Italy."

"Yes. I was born and raised in San Gimignano, Tuscany. Considering how close Italy is to Africa, I am surprised anyone would be surprised by a Black Italian, honestly," Mauricio said flatly. "Unfortunately, they are almost as racist there as you are here." He threw Seth a pointed look.

Seth's glare steeled, and he drew in a breath. "Well, why are you here?"

Ranjan, Darren, and Jason backed away from Seth. Celeste stepped closer to her husband. Fortune stepped closer to Celeste. No one spoke for a full minute.

Mauricio tapped his chin. "I should say 'because I want to be' and be done with it because I don't entertain rudeness, but I may have to see you again since my wife's best friend is in your orbit, so ... I came here for university, and when I graduated, a start-up technology company recruited me. I worked for them for a few years for pay and stock before they sold their company for a substantial amount. I could have retired at thirty, but I chose to consult with a few companies here and get dual citizenship. Then I met and married my love who loves being here. So, we stay here." He wrapped his arm around Celeste's waist and pulled her close.

Instead of apologizing, Seth nodded in response. He probably didn't even think he'd been rude.

Jason cleared his throat. "How about let's all head to the arcade and get to know each other better," he said, dragging Fortune behind him. The group followed suit down the sidewalk a block to a row of low white buildings nestled between the multi-storied Epicenter and several other high rises.

The venue wasn't just an arcade, it was also a bar and grill, and even had a DJ that spun hits from twenty years ago through the current top ten. The overhead lights seemed dim compared to the bright, colored lights emanating from the games on the right side and the DJ booth in the back left corner of the space. Fortune remembered that the left side held the bar and grill and patrons playing trivia, while the right was packed with arcade-style games.

She directed the group, thinking that everyone would want to start the night somewhere different. She'd made some headway with Dani at the karaoke bar, but it was only when Tina wasn't hovering, so she hoped Tina and Seth would split off to the bar and loosen up, so everyone else could have real fun with the games.

No such luck.

"We should do a team challenge on DanceMania," Dani said, pointing to the huge machine in front of them, blasting snippets of music and flashing pink, green and blue neon lights.

Everyone agreed, getting excited about one-upping a friend or seeing who could dance better than whom.

"Dibs on picking teams," Seth said.

"Why does he always think he can pick the teams?" Celeste loud-whispered to Fortune.

She shrugged and threw Jason a furtive glance.

He sighed and briefly closed his eyes.

"Celeste and Fortune against Dani and Tina!" Seth rubbed his hands together like he'd hatched a surefire plot to bring down an empire. His smug look at Tina, who popped a hip towards him in response, made Fortune want to vomit.

Like with karaoke, Seth was making another judgment based on what he saw outside, not because he knew any of them. He would've learned, if he had gotten to know her or Celeste, that back in their college days, they were clubbing buddies, dancing until the wee hours of the morning, attracting guys who realized after a few songs it was hard to keep up with them, and generally bringing the fun at whatever club they entered. And while they weren't those young girls anymore, they'd always been plus size. Moving hadn't been a problem then, and even though they were a little slower now, so was everyone.

While Dani and Tina may have had that kind of bond, she doubted it. And from Tina's ridiculous performance at karaoke night, she was pretty sure Tina could dance about as good as Phil Collins in the 80s.

Fortune glanced at her BFF and winked.

Celeste winked in return.

The game was a two-player team style, so Fortune gave Dani and Tina the first go. After making it through several songs, they managed to rack up a respectable score before game over.

Celeste and Fortune stepped on DanceMania at the same moment, already projecting the air of dancing champions.

Someone from the group gasped.

"We're not club-hopping twenty-year-olds anymore," Fortune whispered.

"Neither are they," Celeste said. She dropped two tokens in the machine, and the round started. The first couple of moves were tricky, but after they got into a rhythm. Fortune and Celeste were hitting their marks like pros. After only a few minutes, they had surpassed Dani and Tina and collected a few onlookers to boot.

Fortune hopped off the DanceMania machine with a small bounce, high-fived her best friend and shook her hips. "I believe that's a win!" She bowed, laughing, then shook her way into her boyfriend's arms. She and Celeste had beaten Dani and Tina by over 10,000 points.

Ranjan kissed Darren on the cheek. "Love ya, babe, but I've got to go with Fortune next round. She's good at this, and you know I have to win."

Seth snarled. "I didn't know big people could move like that."

"You've never been to a Rogue Storm concert, have you?" Fortune shot back.

Jason laughed.

Fortune shot him a look, and he toned it down but not by much. She shook her head.

Ranjan and Fortune deposited their tokens and started the game. Music filled the air once again, and the dancing pair were hitting the toe touches and spinning and flourishing like they had been doing this for years. The group cheered them on, except for Tina, who was seething in the background and Seth, who had disappeared into the arcade. When the selection came to an end, they had the second-highest score right under some team with the initials "EE" and "LF."

Fortune decided to call it a night. Tina scrambled to find Seth, and they exited the way they came in—as a group—with Tina and Seth trailing a half a block behind the rest of the friends.

"Tonight was awesome," Jason said when they arrived back at their meeting spot, then kissed Fortune full and hard. He was warm and vibrating as he encircled her in his arms.

"Ugh, get a room." Graham laughed and hiccupped. Clearly, he'd had too much to drink, which was evidenced in the last two rounds of DanceMania where he'd not only lost spectacularly to both Ranjan and Fortune but almost fell off the machine in his single-player battle with Tina.

Jason peered into Fortune's eyes. "We plan to."

The lust-filled stare made her melt in his embrace. Who were these people again?

"Dani, make sure he gets home, okay?" Jason called over his shoulder, not taking his eyes off Fortune.

"You know I will. Night, everyone." Dani waved at the group that was slowly disbanding and taking the elevator or hiking the ramp through the parking lot to their cars.

Fortune could almost feel the weight of Jason's gaze as she got in the passenger side of his work truck, holding on to the grab bar and swinging her lower half in. Her face heated as she looked over her shoulder at him. "What's the deal with you, Jason? Never seen a big woman get in a truck before? You know I did this earlier tonight."

"I wasn't as horny then as I am now."

She cackled.

He merely smiled, faking like he was a sweet, innocent boy. "Tonight was fun, wasn't it?" Jason slid his palm over hers. He drummed his fingers over the back of her hand in rhythm to the music her mind registered at that moment. Had he been playing music the whole time?

"Yeah, so much fun. I think everyone had a good time."

"This was a great plan." He kissed the back of her clasped hand and smiled without taking his eyes from the road. "You're spending the night at my place, right?"

The vibes came off him like radio waves. This group date thing was working—at least in his opinion—and he wasn't just happy, he was ecstatic. And ecstatic somehow led to horny. With all the dancing and laughing and rushes of endorphins and all that, it made sense. She was giddy, too, not only about how the night went but that she'd made significant headway getting to know Dani. They weren't exactly friends yet, but they were civil, sometimes even cordial. And something about that made Fortune as happy as Jason seemed to be.

The same couldn't be said for Tina or Seth. At least Tina joined in and refrained from spouting rude and insulting remarks like Seth did. He was stubbornly and blatantly showing his stripes at every event so far, and Jason was dismissing it as Seth being Seth. He wasn't really part of the group; he was "just the keg guy".

That line needed to be retired.

Jason's fingers unclasped from hers and traced an invisible pattern up and down her arm. He was in that zone of his—confident, charming, and all kinds of goosebumpy goodness oozing from him. She wanted to feel the same, but there was one thing blocking it. "What do you think about Seth?"

"I try not to think about him. As usual, he was rude. I like the way you put him in his place, though." He glanced at her, all swoony bedroom eyes. "It was hella hot."

She cracked a smile. Dang it, this man. Doing everything to make her feel like a goddess, like a brassy boss.

But she couldn't shake that nagging insecure thought that sooner or later, he'd have to choose between them. And those choices never ended in her favor.

She'd been dumped for friends before. Dates had been canceled for guys' nights out. Her texts weren't readily answered. And then there was her previous boyfriend Thomas, who thought they were an indoor sport—she'd never met any of his friends.

For once, she had a good guy who treated her right, who acknowledged her in public, who had even said I love you and meant it. Jason wasn't ashamed of her, or confused about his feelings for her, or didn't put his friends ahead of her. She wasn't going to give him up, just because his friend didn't like Black women. That wasn't her problem; it was his. She wanted this man, and she deserved him. She'd proven that to Tina and Dani—not that she needed to, but still. And while Tina hadn't conceded, at least she wasn't actively battling Fortune. And Dani had become almost accepting.

Seth brought tension and strain to the group dynamic. But why would he do that if his friend was happy being with her?

Jason might have to choose between them, and she didn't want to lose him to that racist jackass. Moreover, she didn't want Jason to lose himself and his happiness to hold on to a friend out of obligation. But when it got down to it, Seth and Jason had been friends for over twenty years. Guys wouldn't throw that away for a girl. But if she was *the* girl ... This time she wasn't going to lose, especially not to some racist jerk.

Jason has to pick me.

She'd never gone up against a longtime friend in a battle of worth with the prize being Jason. But he wouldn't pick between a friendship with Seth and a relationship with her. Those were different things.

But if Jason was going to have to choose, Fortune was going to make it as difficult a choice as she could. If they thought she was a big Sapphire, tonight she would be the biggest Sapphire ever. Little did they know Jason was turned on by her brassiness. Her sexy snarkiness would have him crawling, begging, demanding to get inside her and never leave.

No way Seth could compete with that.

She stilled his touch and then reached up and ran her fingers raggedly through his hair as they sped down the interstate back across town. His grin was full of lust, and she prayed hers matched. When would she get to the point where she stopped having to prove herself?

Thirteen

Jason

TONIGHT WAS SO MUCH fun. The way Fortune had become comfortable around his friends was amazing. And he would never be mad when she won a game, even against him, because she always jumped up and down. *You're a perv, Reed.* No, he just thought this woman was the sexiest thing on the planet, and the bouncing boobs were a part of it. More than that, she'd been having fun. She hadn't outright said it yet, but who'd doubt it? Her excitable chatter, dancing with her friends and one of his, and that smile that melted all his frustration away shone brighter than the sun. He loved it so much.

As he stood next to her on the tiny, cramped front porch, pride and appreciation shifted to desire and hunger. Her scent mixed with the air, and for a moment, he thought he was in a field of vanilla bean orchids. He wanted to dive into her, as if it were summer, and she was the only pool in the city that could squelch his heat.

"I want you, Fortune." He held her so close they were breathing the same air. He bent and sniffed her neck and then licked his way from her ear to her collar bone, so intoxicated by her scent that he was sure he would be drunk before they made it inside.

"That's evident," she answered, slipping a hand between them and running it down the front of his pants. "I'm here for it."

Mrs. Kosinski's dog yapped loudly, very close to them. They looked over and saw the dog's muzzle pressed to the window with the curtain draped over most of him as he barked.

Fortune giggled.

Jason rolled his eyes. "That damned dog is a blocker for sure."

"Don't think anything could block that freight train in your pants." She doubled over in laughter as he hurried to unlock the door and yank her inside.

"Are you making fun of me?"

She pouted and batted her eyelashes. "Can't take a joke, Mister Reed? Aw, is Mister Reed upset?"

Why did she have to be hot no matter what role she played? Heat crept up his neck, and her eyes went there. Then, her hand as she pulled him down for a kiss. Her soft, plush lips skated over his before pressing deep. She trailed kisses down his chin and then to his neck, cooling the heat there but warming him in other areas. Her tongue licked a path down to his collar bone before she stepped back.

"I think we need to cool off." She smirked. "I'm going to take a shower."

"What kind of tricks are you playing, woman?" His voice was a low rasp.

"No tricks." She raised her eyebrows. "Might be treats, though." She turned and headed up the stairs. "Lock the door."

He obeyed and then followed.

When he made it to his bedroom, she was already in the bathroom with the door closed, humming some song, and as he stopped to listen, his insides warmed. Her melodic alto made him think about warm honey sliding down the side of a jar. He wanted to stick his hand in that jar and into the slick smoothness of her.

"I'm coming in." He went to the door and turned the knob slowly in case she needed a minute.

She'd turned the water on and gotten partially undressed, her shirt and socks thrown over her sneakers in the corner. He hadn't even thought about what she'd been wearing, but now he wanted to see every piece as it came off. Was this what it was like to be horny and high on a successful night? He wished he could save the sensation for later.

She shielded her bra-covered chest with her arm. As if he hadn't seen those before. "Geez Louise, Jason! You're over forty. Shouldn't you be taking a little blue pill or something?"

His palms itched to touch her, pull her close while she was being the sassy temptress he craved.

He egged her on. "Stop being so sexy then."

She deflected. "No can do. That's not how I roll."

"How about you roll on out of those clothes?"

She cackled. "Wow, gag."

He devoured her insult and advanced on her, nuzzling her neck and tickling her until she was a puddle in his arms. He tickled her right out of the rest of her clothes—bra, jeans, and even those cute fire-engine red boy shorts that barely covered her bottom.

He guided her to the shower. "Get in. I want to see you." The command came out so low and guttural, he sounded more bear than human. Gooseflesh raised her skin underneath his fingers.

She stepped under the running water, then glanced back at him with a sultry stare. Immediately, he regretted being fully dressed and on the other side of the shower's glass wall. Water cascaded over her body like the hands of a gentle lover, and he became both jealous and aroused. The soft mounds of her breasts and rounded curves of her torso made him so hard that being inside his jeans was painful. He took them off while he watched her lather up. She was humming again, and a warmth spread through his chest. He ditched his shirt as she stood out of the way of the spray and covered herself in suds.

He shuffled closer until he was pressed against the glass. Was this a tease or torture? "Fortune, sweetie. Let me see you."

She stepped under the water. The white bubbles slid down her smooth brown skin with the water, and he went rock hard. She's first, he mentally chanted, but he couldn't stop staring, urgent lust coursing through him. His fantasy was right there in front of him. He slid a hand in his boxer briefs, but that wasn't going to be enough. Now that he was with her, nothing he did without her was ever enough.

He shed the boxer briefs and rounded the shower wall, pressing her front to his. She was soft and slick against his solid frame. "I couldn't wait."

"What is with you? You people always wanting what you want when you want it."

"Did you just say 'you people' to me?"

She inhaled sharply. "I said what I said."

His hand settled in the crook of her neck, his thumb stroking her collarbone. "What do you mean, 'you people'? White guys? That phrase hurts me as much as it hurts you."

She jutted her chin in defiance. "You don't know how much I hurt."

He hadn't until maybe this moment, and even then, he wasn't sure. Her brazenness and smooth façade hid a lot of things.

But lust and desire were overwhelming his rational thought, and he didn't want to debate. He just wanted inside her. "I'm not Graham, and I'm sure as hell not Seth." His hand slid down her slick skin, and he watched the water cascade over her breasts and down her body. He tweaked a nipple.

She gasped.

"I want you. Me. And I came to get what's mine." He backed her against the white tile and kneeled in front of her, his hand completing its journey to rest between her thighs.

"Like that's not possessive." Her words dripped with sarcasm and need.

He kissed her hip and slid a finger into her. "Tell me you don't want it."

"I—" Her breath hitched.

"Don't lie. You're wet."

"It's a running shower. We both are."

"Now, you're just playing." He slid another finger inside her.

She bit her lip as their gazes connected.

God, she was so sexy. He wanted to tease her like this for hours just to watch pleasure register on her face. If only his body would let him. "Tell me you don't want this." He slowly pumped his fingers in and out of her.

She answered with a moan and closed her eyes.

He kissed his way from her hip to the inside of her thigh. "I'm not 'you people'. Who am I, Fortune?"

She mumbled something unintelligible as she bucked against his hand.

He sped up the pace. "Say my name, Fortune."

She was tightening around him, worked up to almost her peak.

He loved seeing her unravel like this, releasing the protective armor and just being her, the woman she was meant to be. He thumbed her clit, and her hands went into his hair. "Say my name."

"Jason!" Her back arched, and she nudged him closer.

There was one thing he knew would send her spilling over the edge. He replaced his thumb with his mouth, licking and sucking until she vibrated with an orgasm. She repeated his name as she peaked, and he thought about honey again as he tasted her.

Fourteen

Fortune

JASON ROSE TO STANDING, towering over Fortune with a big grin.

"Smug jerk," she huffed, barely able to catch her breath. She sagged against the wall.

He laughed like a maniac. Then he advanced on her, his manhood hard against her stomach, lifted her leg, and wound it around his waist.

"Um, what are you doing?"

He raised an eyebrow. "What do you think?"

She put a hand on his chest. "I need you to put all of that," she gestured towards his penis, "in a condom. I'm not having your giant baby just because you wanna have hot shower sex."

He reared back for a moment giving her a look that said *are you for real?* Then he shook his head and grinned again. "Why are you calling my future babies giants?"

"Look at you, crazy man."

He guffawed and nodded. "I accept that." He kissed her, then let go of her leg and went in search of a condom, leaving a wet trail behind him.

Fortune adjusted the water temperature and stood in the spray. His absence registered immediately. So, she perched a foot on the tiled shower bench and reached between her legs. As sure as she was about her own ministrations, there was nothing better than a guy knowing how to use his hand to bring her to the precipice of pleasure. Correction, there was nothing better than Jason's skilled hands. Well, his tongue and his penis weren't bad, either.

She closed her eyes and leaned back against the tile, her fingers gliding deftly in, out, and around. Her thoughts were full of him and his long, thick fingers, the rough calluses adding friction where hers didn't. She hummed as she en-visioned what was to come but made sure that she wouldn't until he got back, until he was inside her.

Jason swore and startled her.

She blinked wildly, reorienting herself to where she was. Her lip quirked up as she connected with his gaze. "What?"

"The only thing sexier than my hand there is yours."

Hmm. Noted.

Apparently, there was some difference in perspective. "I can think of something else sexier."

She ogled him as he stalked towards her. Manliness radi-ated off him, from his broad shoulders to his solid torso, to his tree trunk legs. She couldn't wait to have her hands all over him.

But then he said, "Turn around."

She was taken aback. "What?"

He grabbed her waist and nudged her into a pivot. "Turn. Around. I want you from behind."

Not her best angle. Her backside was unremarkable—flat, wide, and dimpled with cellulite. And no one wanted to see back fat. She wasn't ashamed of her body, but she also knew its sexiest parts, and these were not.

Her defiant swagger that fed off lust and Jason's cockiness faded a little. She slung her arm across her breasts, unsure of what to do with her hands, now that she couldn't touch him. "Um ..."

"You're overthinking." He pressed her against the wall, his hand tracing down the center of her back. He teased her into an arch, and her backside rose.

Fortune hesitated, looking across her shoulder up into his eyes. "Um, that's not ..."

He stepped back for a moment. "Are you uncomfortable?"

She sighed. "I'm fine. I ... It's just not sexy," she blurted.

"The hell it isn't." He rubbed a hand over her bottom, then kneeled and placed a kiss on each cheek. An instant flame lit in her core. She'd never been kissed there before. It was nice.

He stood and leaned in and whispered gruffly. "How about you let me be the judge of what I think is sexy for once? Spread your legs."

She widened her stance, the steamy air of the shower doing little to cool her.

He ran a finger up and down her seam, swirling around the shower's moisture and her own and drawing jagged whimpers out of her. He growled low in his throat. "Damn, Fortune."

It was tawdry and raw. Even though she'd just showered, she felt dirty, exposed, and so hot she thought she would burst into flames. Good thing there was running water nearby. She could only register the joke for a second before Jason rained more sensations on her—pricks of delicious pain as he spread her wider, pressure as he teased her opening, weight as he leaned on her back and pressed his lips to her ear.

"Stop overthinking. What's the problem?"

Desperation ate away at her confidence and resolve, and no matter how much Jason validated her, it didn't erase what other boyfriends had done and said. And if she couldn't keep them interested, how was she going to keep Jason interested enough to pick her over a twenty–plus year friendship?

"It's ... no one's ever thought my ass in the air was sexy." Fortune took a deep breath. Now that she'd said it out loud, it seemed silly. She was trying too hard, and for what? So she could one-up Seth? So Jason would choose her?

"I do. And I'm not the only one." His penis twitched.

She was reminded that he'd asked for this. And he wouldn't ask her to do something that would turn him off. And the hard, panting man behind her was very much on.

"Now that you've stalled enough to catch your breath, may I please get inside you before I explode?"

She laughed, and it came out all husky and breathy. "I wasn't stalling."

He released her hold on her breasts as he inched inside, holding her wrist against the wall. "You were." His voice was gravelly and deep. "Because you know you're sexy as hell." He pressed her front to the wall, his other hand cupping her sex. He thumbed her clit, and she moaned and bowed away from the wall, pushing him in deeper. He groaned.

They traded back and forths, Fortune challenging Jason with every volley, and Jason returning with fire, crumbling her walls of resolve until she begged him not to stop. Each thrust was a delicious ache, filling her more, stretching her wider, pressing her against the cool tile that was the only relief from the steamy heat of their bodies and the shower.

With her legs spread wide, her breasts thrust into his palms, she was determined to imprint this night on his mind as long as she could. This was the one thing Seth couldn't give Jason; he had to remember that. There was no way she was giving this up. She wouldn't give him up.

The edges of Fortune's orgasm were tingling in her muscles. It was like a clanging alarm, signaling she was almost out of time.

"Come for me, baby," Jason coaxed.

"No, I—not yet." She tried to breathe evenly and tamp down the building urge, as if more time like this would sear her importance into his memory. She went from whimpering to frantic, crying out in desperate pleasure. "Jason! Oh God, I can't stop. Jason!"

"I'm here, sweetie. What is it? What do you need?"

Overwhelmed by sensations and hormones zipping through her, Fortune screamed, "I need you to pick me!"

His answer was strained as he barely kept his own orgasm at bay. "Always. I will always pick you."

They came apart together, both sinking to their knees and panting heavily. Jason held Fortune against his front, one arm around her waist, the other across her collarbone. His heaves pressed against her back, and he still pulsed inside her. Was he protecting her or holding on for dear life? Who could tell?

Fortune leaned back across Jason's chest and laid a hand on his cheek.

He planted small kisses on her neck and shoulder. "My back is going to hate me tomorrow. Worth it, though."

"We've gotta get out of here. The water's getting cold."

They disentangled themselves, and Fortune gave herself one last cold rinse while Jason dealt with the condom. He wrapped them each in a towel, and they climbed into bed, sitting and leaning against the headboard, Jason cuddling Fortune's back.

"You okay?" Jason asked.

"Yeah, I'm fine."

"So, what was that?"

"Some massively hot shower sex." Fortune's tone was flippant, but her voice cracked at the end. She hoped he hadn't heard the waver and would leave her alone about it. Talking through her screaming climax confessions right now had about as much appeal as sitting on a cactus. But when he turned her to face him, she went along willingly.

"You know what I mean. About picking you? Why did you need to ask?"

She slid down in the bed until her head hit the pillow, and she closed her eyes. "I didn't! I just ... Let's drop this."

Jason slid down beside her. He kissed her forehead. "Is this a Marshall thing?"

She hadn't thought about her high school crush turned creep in months. Not since Jason pretended not to remember his name. She was way past her hurt over Marshall rating her body a four and a half. She had bigger hurdles to overcome. "No. It's not a Marshall thing."

After a few moments, Jason asked, "Does this have to do with Seth?"

Fortune didn't answer.

Fifteen

Jason

T HOUGH FORTUNE'S ORIGINAL PLAN was for Jason to drop her off at the end of the night, the shower sex rendered them incapable of moving from his bed until morning. The subsequent delivery of Beans & Bread's cinnamon rolls and coffee kept Fortune satisfied, in his house and back in his bed that morning and, after agreeing they both needed a couple of days to themselves, they stayed in bed for most of the rest of the weekend. They'd only gotten up once on Sunday, determined to binge-watch a few hours of *Titans* and then people-watch a few hours at Freedom Park. They'd made it through a half an episode before they were in each other's arms and then back upstairs to his bed.

After their last love-making session, tangled in sheets and each other, Fortune stated, "I'm not going to take anyone's last name if I ever get married."

Jason stared at her as if she had grown a third arm. They hadn't been talking about marriage nor had they ever talked about marriage. Even though he'd already imagined it multiple times. Had they gotten so close that she could read his mind? "And you're letting me know this, why?"

"In case it's a deal breaker," she responded. She looked at him as if she were daring him to refute her point that the sky was blue.

Instead, he answered, "It's not a deal breaker."

She shifted to face him. "It's not? Why not?"

"Because the only thing that matters is if you say yes when I ask you to marry me, and say I do when we face each other at the end of the aisle."

Fortune was quiet for a moment, a contemplative look on her face. "Are we talking about us getting married?"

Jason sighed and smiled, a single eyebrow raised. "You brought it up. Are we?"

"If we are, then that means you have to meet my family. And I'm not sure I want that yet."

"Makes me want to continue this even further." He rubbed his hands together like a cheesy, poor imitation of a villain. "What's up with your family?"

"Nothing. They will eat you alive, though. Haven't brought home a boyfriend yet that they haven't. My mom especially."

Jason gaped, wide-eyed. "How many potential fiancés have you brought home to meet your family?"

"Oh!" She laughed. "No fiancés. I'm talking about regular boyfriends. Guys I've seriously dated. But they could have been the one. If Mom hadn't taken them to that CIA black site for interrogation." Now she rubbed her hands together villain-style.

Jason stared warily at her. "You're joking, right?"

She shrugged and grinned.

Jason grabbed his tablet from the nightstand, and they spent the afternoon looking at wedding rings online. Fortune had a sense of what she wanted and what she thought looked good, but it was clear she hadn't really thought about wedding rings. She did have a few Pinterest boards where she'd pinned what she liked for wedding themes and décor. It was very arts and crafts, as if she were creating a look for someone else—showing a potential client the possibility of a sweetly decorated wedding—not that she could or would have this for herself. Something she said when they were working through their first rough patch struck him then: "Guys like you don't take girls like me home to their parents, unless they're trying to give them heart attacks by showcasing their 'bad choices.'"

Despite what she'd said, he'd have no problems taking her home to meet his family, and they'd most likely love her and welcome her. Well, most of them would. He wasn't sure about his dad. Jim Reed hadn't really seemed on board with anything Jason did these days, and he didn't want to even think about why. Every time his mind went there, he'd see his father's disapproving stare while Jason fiercely argued to go to Arizona State and major in Construction Science. Nothing between him and his father would change, so there was no point. His dad would come around, even if he didn't wholeheartedly approve.

Fortune wasn't a bad choice; she was the best thing that ever happened to him. His father would see that, just like his friends were. He was sure of it.

The time had been so blissfully uneventful that Jason didn't want to leave the cocoon of love, IPA beer, and half-eaten pizza. He wanted to stay so much that when he finally awoke Monday morning after turning off the first alarm and snoozing countless times on the second, he found himself running late and wishing that weekends had three days instead of two.

Fortune didn't have to be at work until ten that day, but he liked to stop at Beans & Bread and then his office before arriving at the job site by seven-thirty every day to run down the list of to-dos before the crew started work. He could've had Austin read the task list just the same, but surveying the clean, bright faces of his crew before they became dusty and worn with the messy tasks of the day was energizing.

He was just going to have to skip the office. Coffee was non-negotiable.

He scrambled to get ready while Fortune dragged herself from the bed to the bathroom and followed him to the car, clad in her jeans from Friday night and one of his old t-shirts. She complained that his shirts were two sizes too small but put it on anyway. He stopped briefly to stare at the Captain America logo stretched across her chest.

Jesus, he was like a horny teenager when he saw her in tight clothes. While his bros were at karaoke discussing the efficacy of all the new erectile dysfunction and artificial testosterone drugs on the market, he'd been using expendable effort to tamp down his excitement at seeing Fortune on stage in tight jeans, twerking against Louis.

"I'm late." He shook his head and hoped the action would refocus him. They were in front of Beans & Bread, and he was already out of the car. "Do you want anything?"

"I'm going in."

He wanted to ask, *looking like that?*, but he didn't dare. It wasn't because he thought she looked bad. She didn't. In fact, with his shirt clinging to her curves, no makeup, and a still sleepy expression, she had that frumpled, sexy look he loved. It was because, if he didn't point it out now, she would berate him later about letting her go in public wearing a "walk of shame" outfit, even though she didn't feel one inkling of shame. He'd deflect. "I don't know if we have time."

She motioned to the door. From beyond the all-glass storefront, he saw the sparseness of the coffee shop. The morning rush hadn't started yet.

He took her hand and went inside. His favorite barista was at the counter and smiled when he saw them walk in. "Hi, Jason! The usual?" he asked, even though he'd already plucked a large cup from the dispenser and was writing his name on it.

"Hi, Craig. Yes, and whatever she wants."

Fortune ordered a large hazelnut coffee with two shots of chocolate syrup and extra whipped cream, and a cinnamon roll. "It's my new favorite breakfast," she said, looking up at him and raising an eyebrow.

They'd started Saturday morning sipping their coffees in bed, but then she'd gotten whipped cream on her nose, and then he explored the idea of what she'd taste like with cinnamon roll icing all over her, and the morning-after coffee turned into a passionate appeal for a weekend of ingesting calories and burning them off minutes later.

Craig whipped up the coffees in record time—probably because he eyed the crowd about to descend on him for the morning rush—and another barista boxed the cinnamon roll and an avocado toast topped with egg for Jason, and they headed out with only seconds to spare before the cranky Monday morning hoard burst through the doors.

Jason dropped off Fortune with a kiss, skipped the stop at his office, and made it to the job site just in time to run through the day's list. One of his welders was out with the flu, which would slow down the work, but he had more than the usual number of day laborers, so they could get most of the debris cleanup done ahead of schedule.

Austin walked over to Jason as the crew went to work. "Slow start this morning. Miss Tatas kept you up late?"

Jason's eyes narrowed, but his mouth formed a smug smile. "You know her name's Fortune."

"She'd definitely got you acting like you just won one."

A guffaw escaped at the same time a warm flush crept up his neck. "I have. She's amazing." He went over their time in the shower and the weekend afterward in his mind, appreciating how much she'd come out of her shell since they'd started dating eight months ago.

When she'd said, "I need you to pick me", though, it struck him as odd. The worrisome itch of it wouldn't let him go, but he hadn't thought to go back and asked her what it meant. Why would she think he wouldn't pick her? And more importantly, pick her for what?

"Whoa, boss. You sure about that?"

His expression must have changed. Jason touched his cheek as if he could feel what Austin had seen. "Oh! Yeah, yeah. I'm sure. I was just ..." He trailed off, not certain how to finish the sentence.

Austin scratched his bearded chin so hard the rasp was audible above the pneumatic nail guns several of the guys were using.

"Don't look at me like that. I do think Fortune's amazing. I just don't know why she doesn't believe me when I tell her that."

"Probably because you look at her like that when you do." He pointed and circled the air in front of Jason's face.

He slapped away Austin's finger, and the two got back to work. Jason pushed Fortune's plea out of his thoughts, but the nagging worry that he missed something crucial she was saying stayed with him for the rest of the day.

Sixteen

Fortune

J ASON, FORTUNE, CELESTE, MAURICIO, Ranjan, Darren, Dani,
and Graham were huddled together in front of the movie
theater, about to go in, when someone in the parking lot
shouted, "Eastcoasters!"

Fortune winced at the voice. It was Seth. "I thought you
said he wasn't coming," she whispered to Jason.

"He wasn't," he whispered back. "This was the last message I got from him." He flashed a text screen to Fortune,
and she read Seth's last words:

Not going to make it. Have fun.

And they had been having fun. They'd attempted a sort of
re-do of the dinner of microaggressions, opting for a fast,
casual Peruvian place across the street from the theater.
The four couples sat across from each other, and though
she thought facing Dani and Graham would make for an
excruciating experience, it had actually been fun.

"So, let's address the elephant in the room," Dani started while they waited on their food to arrive. "Fortune, you had a crush on this schmuck right here?" She nudged Graham, who rolled his eyes at his girlfriend.

"In my younger days, obviously a misguided, misspent youth."

The group laughed.

Graham looked mildly offended.

"But seriously," Fortune continued. "You two are perfect for each other. And I got the guy who's perfect for me." She looked into Jason's eyes, filled with passion and love only for her. Her neck and face heated as her own love for him bloomed, begging to be shown. "At the time, I just needed a date for this gala. I wasn't thinking about falling in love. And here I am, totally smitten with this lumberjack."

They kissed amid a table of hoots and jeers, but when Fortune looked around, everyone else had the same look of passion in their eyes for their partner. She beamed at the way they were coming together, making her feel like they were a part of something wonderful.

That feeling lasted until Seth shouted at them. Tension among the friends that was all but erased moments before was now at a DEFCON 2 level as he strutted up to the group with a scantily clad Tina in tow. Her hair was slightly frizzy, one side of her shirt was higher than the other, and her lipstick needed to be reapplied. They'd obviously been making out before they got out of the car to meet their friends.

Jason left Fortune's side to greet Seth. "Dude, I thought you said you weren't going to make it."

"Plans changed. Got a lot more free time now, so why not spend it with my long-time friends?" He glanced at Fortune pointedly, then made his way around the circle, doling out bro hugs to fellow Eastcoasters and leaving confused faces in his wake.

"The Black Italian is here! How ya doing, buddy?" Seth attempted to bro hug Mauricio, but he took a step back. Seth held up both his hands as if to say, "no harm, no foul", and went back to Tina, yanking her to him by the waist. "Are we ready to see these guys blast each other out of the sky or what?" He laughed and led the way inside the theater.

After a minor skirmish at the ticket kiosk where Seth insisted that Jason pay for his and Tina's ticket since he'd paid for everyone else's, they were behind the velvet rope and in the middle of another contentious battle.

"Tina and I want to sit in the middle row."

Jason sighed. "Seth, we had this figured out before you got here. It's me, Fortune, Celeste, and Mauricio on the first row; Dani, Graham, Ranjan, and Darren on the second row. You and Tina are behind Ranjan and Darren."

"That's too far back for me. I'm not pulling out my glasses just to see a superhero movie with y'all." He turned to Ranjan. "Switch places with me, dude."

"No," Ranjan answered. "You're causing commotion for no reason. This is a large screen in a relatively small theater. You might not even need your glasses."

"I'm going to the bathroom while you guys duke this out," Fortune told Jason. When he nodded, she pulled Celeste by the hand to the dual entrance bathroom that reminded Fortune of being at the airport.

When they entered on one side, Dani and Tina were already at the sinks near the other entrance chattering in hushed voices, despite the bathroom being almost empty. Fortune and Celeste halted by the makeup mirrors, not wanting to disturb them but ready to eavesdrop.

"What's going on with you, Tina?" Dani said, a stripe of worry on top of concern on her face. "You look car-sexed and crazed."

Tina shook her head and wiped off the remnants of her lipstick with a paper towel. "I'm fine. Seth is just being a little extra right now. It's nothing that he can't fix."

"He's putting everyone on edge."

"He's not doing anything that interloper Fortune hasn't already done to this group. She's a menace."

Dani sighed. "She's not a menace. She's actually kind of nice. And she's Jason's girlfriend, so there's that."

"Maybe she shouldn't be Jason's girlfriend. Maybe he's too blindsided by lust to really see what a problem he's causing." Tina reapplied the blood-red lipstick in two slashes, threw it in her microscopic purse, and snapped it shut.

"I think you're the one being blindsided, Tina. Seth's got a few screws loose."

Tina laughed wryly. "You're right about that."

The two left the bathroom, and Fortune and Celeste stared at each other with incredulous looks before scrambling to get in the stalls and back out before the movie began.

Even though superheroes were blasting each other to kingdom come, Seth and Tina were plastered to each other's faces, making out like they were at least twenty-five years younger. What Fortune thought would be a good time, now that everyone was starting to get along, turned into an uncomfortable peep show no one wanted.

Seth had gotten his way with the seating arrangements, sitting beside Graham and in front of Ranjan. He'd managed to stay quiet only until the title credits, and then he created a general disturbance throughout the movie, talking back loudly to the screen, laughing in inappropriate places, and slurping loudly on a large fountain drink. And now he was using the theater as his bedroom.

Graham shoved him in the side. "Dude! Cut it!"

The couple straightened, and everyone else settled back in for the movie's finish. But before the end credits started to roll, Seth and Tina exited the theater and didn't return.

When the rest of the group exited, everyone glanced around, half-looking for the raucous duo, half-hoping they wouldn't find them. They were gone. As they gathered again outside the theater and said goodbyes, the mood was less full of love and joy than it had been earlier.

Fortune was chagrined as she hugged her friends and thanked them for joining. "I'm not apologizing for Seth, but I hope that wasn't a waste of a good night out."

"Getting to hang out with my bestie is never a waste of time. Besides, dinner was delightful. Jason's friends have accepted you. Well, most of them."

Mauricio clasped her forearm, and the three of them huddled together. "Everyone's on your side except that blond guy," he said, his voice haunted like he was the sole person with common sense in a horror movie. "Don't let them make excuses for him. He's a racist jerk. They need to drop him, or he's going to force Jason to leave you."

Fortune breathed in deeply, letting Mauricio's advice linger in the air and her mind as her friends said their goodbyes and each couple went their separate ways into the parking lot.

Jason asked, "Do you want to come back to my place? I can drop you off in the morning."

The hopeful look in his eyes made her cringe inside, but she was not in the mood to be with anyone else tonight. "I'm not going to be good company. I'd rather go home."

Despite the resigned look on his face, he kissed her on the cheek and gave her a long hug before they got in the car.

The pair were silent for the first part of the ride across town. Fortune wondered if Jason was disappointed with how the night had turned out and if he was rethinking his plans for more group dates. She, however, was stuck on Seth's behavior. She would never understand why Seth's life goal seemed to be to put her in this small, societal box so he could ridicule her. From the moment they interacted at Silver Foxes as strangers to now as his longtime friend's girlfriend, Seth was working his hardest at making Fortune uncomfortable. But nothing he did had or would have any effect on her.

It did, however, make an impact on the group. Jason, Graham, and Dani were ill at ease each time he disparaged Fortune, and it created a sympathetic but obvious distance between her and the rest of the group. Maybe that was his point. Break her away from his friends to break her and Jason up.

Jason mused about Seth's motivation, too. "Wonder what Seth's issue was tonight? Everything was great until he showed up."

"Mhmm," she said.

"I've got to talk to him. Find out where his head is. He's never acted like this before. It must be something with his job; I think there was some kind of promotion? Or not."

"Why? Don't you know where his head is? He obviously doesn't like these group dates, and he's acting out."

"But this is weird. Even for him."

She disagreed. This wasn't weird. He didn't want her here. Whether it was racism, or fatphobia, or just plain dislike for her, he wanted her gone. And he was doing everything he could to fulfill his wish.

Seventeen

Jason

EVERYTHING WAS GOING GREAT. Granted, Seth had been unusually stubborn and an all-around jackass at the movies, but everyone else seemed to have fun. Except for the night before, the group dates were a hit. They'd brought his friends closer to Fortune, and they'd made his relationship with Fortune better. They were more comfortable with each other, more affectionate, and the sex ... wow. He remembered their night together after the second date, and a wide grin crept to his lips. Since then, they'd even talked about marriage. Granted, he'd been imagining their married life for months already, but when she brought it up and even agreed to go ring shopping, Jason was sure it was because she could see herself in his life, too.

So, when she'd texted, *I'm coming over. We need to talk,* it caught him off-guard. Those were never good words.

He scanned the past few weeks to pinpoint why she'd "need to talk." Had one of his friends done something they hadn't addressed and resolved? Had he done something?

The doorbell rang.

He startled, then shook his head, chiding himself. Get it together, Reed. You're worrying about nothing.

She stepped across the threshold almost timidly and avoided his gaze, but she did rear up and give him a quick peck on the cheek before crossing the foyer to her favorite place on the sofa.

He couldn't read her, so he closed the door slowly, went to the kitchen, and poured her a glass of Moscato. "What did you want to talk about?"

"These group dates. We should stop doing them."

This is not where he thought she was going. "Why? They're pretty fun. The gang has gotten a chance to know you, and I think they've come around so much since the awkward dinner." He sat the glass of wine in front of her, hoping she'd take a sip and rethink this. His plan was working! She just needed to give it a few more dates.

"You're right. Most of them have come around. Dani sometimes even makes small talk with me, and I thought she'd be hashtag Team Tina forever. But one person is never going to be won over, so we should stop trying."

Seth. Jason slumped on the sofa beside Fortune, unable to articulate any of the myriad thoughts swirling around his brain. He didn't know what was happening with Seth, and he couldn't not invite the guy. Fortune knew that. That's why she suggest ending the group dates altogether.

"Ever since the dance-off at the arcade, where he walked off, I've been thinking about how having him around would affect our relationship. He's done nothing but belittle me. And now, he's just making everyone miserable. Look at how he alienated everyone at the movies. I almost feel sad for Tina." At that sentiment, she threw him a look that made him jump. "I said almost. I mean, what is with him?" She shook her head, her expression pained. "We're talking about maybe getting married? Do you want him at the wedding?"

Jason stared at her. His mouth was open, but nothing was coming out. Obviously, he didn't want him at their wedding if she didn't. But the wedding was nothing but a dream at the moment. And last night's craziness was out of character, even for Seth. This would change; he was sure of it.

She stared back at him, her lips pursed and her eyes squinting in frustration. "I'm so stressed that I'm getting hives. I can't be in the middle of this ... whatever it is. Whatever we were trying to do with this group date thing is not working anymore. We have to end it."

And Jason had thought the marriage talk was a step in the right direction. For Fortune, the massive group dates came rife with more problems and less time to be herself and have fun. All the good signs for him were actually more problems she worried about.

He couldn't believe she was giving up after only three dates. It had been timing with them from the very start. Timing and expectations. The same misfires could be going on here. "Look, I don't know what's going on with Seth. He's usually a jerk, but now he's just gone off the deep end. I think he's struggling with something at work."

Fortune mumbled something.

"What's that?"

"Nothing. Forget it." She turned to face Jason.

He bent his head to his chest and sighed. There was no way around this. No matter what he'd done to bring them all together, they just weren't going to mesh. It would be so much easier if they were pieces of wood and he had construction adhesive.

She kissed his arm and leaned her head on his shoulder. "You're still going to try to fix it, aren't you? It's not a leaky faucet or faulty wiring. It's a human relationship. And sometimes those have to stay broken to function."

His relationship with his dad was broken, but it was functioning—barely. He couldn't let that happen between his friends and his girlfriend. Not if she was going to be his wife. The one thing he hadn't done with his dad, but should have, was to have a serious talk. If he'd made more of an effort to show his father how much he loved construction, maybe their relationship wouldn't have become so messed up.

This time, he would get a moment with Seth—unlike the moment he couldn't get with his father. Jason would meet Seth on his turf, hear him out, and find a way to fix this broken relationship. No, it wasn't construction, but it was what his dad hadn't given him—a chance. "Let me talk to him and see what's really going on there. I know it's not a leaky faucet, but maybe it can be fixed."

If he thought about it, he hadn't actually had a real conversation with Seth since this started. And he'd basically bullied the guy into joining. They'd never been buddies, but they did know what was going on in each other's lives. Or at least he thought so. He should meet him for a beer, just the two of them, no pressure, no dynamics. Seth was better that way. He should probably ask Graham and Ranjan for some perspective first. Fortune was wrong; Jason could still fix this.

As soon as Fortune left, he got a text from Dani.

> Tina wants to talk to you about Seth. Meet tomorrow at Beans & Bread?

Jason wanted to throw his phone across the room. He growled at the screen.

Jason:
> Dani. I can't.

Dani:
> Hear her out.

He paced while raking a hand through his hair. Why was this going so wrong all of a sudden? He could almost hear his dad saying *I told you so*. He went back and picked up his phone and replied to Dani:

Jason:
> Okay, I'll meet her there at 10.

Jason was already halfway through his first cup of coffee when Tina walked in. The coffee shop buzzed even though it was unusually empty. The start of baseball season meant the real rush would come later for picnic baskets full of fresh baked rolls and breads to go with their meats and cheeses from the butcher and cheese shops down the block.

Tina ordered and beelined for Jason. "Hey. Thanks for meeting me."

"What's this about?" Jason surprised himself at how annoyed he sounded, but he couldn't help it. Annoyed was his go-to emotion with this woman.

"You've got to stop with these group dates."

He couldn't believe this. Did everyone hate his idea? "Why?"

"It's Seth."

He smirked. "Big surprise. Did you know he didn't want to do these in the first place?"

"Yeah, he told me. Kind of how we really started talking."

"Well, why would you agree to this? You can't stand to see me happy, so you want to make me miserable? Are you that vindictive?"

Tina straightened in her seat and stuck out her chin. "My world does not revolve around you, Jason. Despite what you believe."

"Why am I here, then? Huh?" Only a few minutes with her, and he was ready to leave. This had been such a waste of time.

"Seth hit me."

He met her stare, not sure he heard what she'd said.

She blinked.

It was like she'd knocked the wind right out of him. "He what?"

"He slapped me. It was backhanded and an accident, but he didn't apologize for it. He was big mad. Seriously angry."

"That doesn't condone him hitting you. Nothing condones him hitting you. Holy hell." He shook his head and massaged his brow. That wasn't what he thought she was going to say.

"Yeah. It's something going on with his job. He'd been working toward a promotion for a few months now, so he was on edge already. Always working late, and he'd met some of the managers a couple of times for a round of golf, but a few days ago, something happened. The Tuesday before the movie, he just stopped. No more talking about a promotion. No talking about work at all.

"He started drinking more and being cruder. And when you sent that text about the movie, he flew into some rage about the UN and everyone getting along. He said he wasn't going to go, but I said I wanted to see the movie, so at the last minute, he said, 'Let's go and ruin it for everyone.'"

"And he pretty much did." His annoyance at her shifted to Seth. What the devil was going on with him? This wasn't jackass behavior; this was a full-on knuckle-dragging monster. "But Tina, what does this have to do with the group dates?"

"I told him I wasn't cool with all of that making out stuff, and we should really give it a rest. That set him off again. He was all hand waving and spouting garbage about American values and people taking away opportunities and other stuff from real Americans. I was trying to calm him down and got in the way of one of his arm flail movements."

She touched her cheek, which Jason now noticed was covered in thick makeup. He stared in awe, unable to discern if the last few minutes of his life had even been real.

"These group dates are making whatever he's going through worse. It's supposed to be a good time, and it's not—not for him. The more of them you do, the worse he's going to get at them. And that's going to make everyone upset. You're breaking your friend group up by continuing these group dates."

He sighed heavily, fighting the sinking feeling in the pit of his stomach. He laid his arm across the table to keep from rubbing a groove in his forehead. Fortune had said as much yesterday, and now Tina, who was Fortune's opposite in so many ways, echoed her words. But what worried him more was Seth's behavior. And now that Tina was taking the brunt of his temper, Jason was concerned. "Tina, you don't have to stay. He's not worth that."

Tina must've taken the gesture as an invitation because she set down her coffee cup and curled both hands around his arm. "What are we going to do about him?"

He hadn't meant to encourage her. "There is no *we* here. *I'm* going to talk to him." Jason slid his arm away as nicely as he could. "Tina, I've already said this. I love Fortune. Period."

"Why her, though? I don't get it. Look at me. Then look at her." She pointed to Fortune's picture on his lock screen.

This damned phone was garnering way too much attention and commentary.

"Why would you even go out with me if *this* is what you wanted?"

"First of all, Fortune is gorgeous. Anyone with eyes can see that. But more importantly, I love her for who she is. Her laugh and her smile make me warm inside. She likes the same types of music I do. She cares about my reasons for substitute teaching and supports them. She's a joy to be around. And she makes the best cheesecake I've ever tasted."

"What are you, a Golden Girl? I can make a cheesecake." Tina pouted.

Ducking his head to hide his smile, he remembered one of his first conversations with Fortune on SwipeMatch, asking which Golden Girl she was. If anything, Tina was smarmy, clingy Stan, Dorothy's ex-husband. "Baking a cheesecake is not the point," he declared. "I love Fortune. You've got to find someone that loves you for you. Not just your looks but the person you are. And stop using Seth to make me jealous. It's not working."

She let out an exaggerated breath and rose to leave. "I *was* using him to make you jealous. But now I'm just concerned about him. Stop with these dates and get your friend back."

She left him sitting with a half-cold cup of coffee and a huge impending sense of doom. First Fortune and now Tina urged him to end the group dates. How do you fix a broken solution?

Eighteen

Jason

Heavy with the weight of Fortune's implications and Tina's narrative, Jason couldn't do more than work and watch TV while he lived with the awful realization that one of his longtime best friends was a racist. Jason had a full week of asking himself soul-probing questions, struggling to piece together feelings with rationality, and worrying about what was to come for the state of all his relationships, platonic and otherwise. How had he not noticed Seth was racist until his Black girlfriend pointed it out?

He had to ask Graham and Ranjan what they thought. What he really wanted to do was interrogate them about the "keg guy" being a lot more and a lot worse than a guy who brings the beer to the party.

Jason:

It's been a rough week. Meet at The Graveyard to blow off some steam?

They agreed.

On Thursday night, baseball fans ready for the season opener of the hometown minor league team filled The Graveyard. Jason never really liked baseball. After Fortune told him that her work bestie's husband was star third-baseman Geronimo Lopez, Jason had watched a few more games to feel what it was like to be three degrees of separation from a minor league baseball celebrity. Still, it wasn't for him. In fact, this whole situation was weird. The gang was here on a Thursday instead of a Friday, the bar was filled with local fans, rabid, rowdy, and all dressed alike—in team colors—and Seth wasn't there. This must've been how the guys felt when he hadn't been around. Everything was just a little bit off.

"So, what's this clandestine get-together all about?" Graham chuckled a little but stopped when he saw Jason's expression. "Okay. This is serious."

"If you can believe this, last week Tina and Fortune told me the same thing—we've got to do away with the group dates."

"I can't believe it," Ranjan's expression was an amalgamation of horror and mischievousness.

Jason scrutinized him. "Yeah, what the hell? I don't know what to think about this. But I guess this is the consensus: I've got to stop the group dates. Both of them attributed it to Seth."

"Well, that's no surprise," Graham said. "He was a total jackass at the movie date."

"Tina said he had a temper tantrum afterwards. That's fixable, I guess." Jason shrugged. "But Fortune said he was a racist."

Graham audibly gasped.

Ranjan snorted.

"I know. She's been saying it for a while in one way or another. I just thought ... I don't know what I thought. But racist? That's bad. That's like Hitler bad. We would've seen that. Right?" Jason was swimming in a jumble of thoughts and possibly drowning a little. Things weren't making sense anymore. Forget fixing anything. Just figuring out the problem was plaguing him now.

"I mean ..." Graham cleared his throat, which was turning bright red. "Um, we're not Black, and she is."

Jason and Ranjan stared at him for a moment, blankness registering on their faces.

"What?" Jason asked.

Graham cleared his throat again, the apples of his cheeks now reddening. "Maybe Fortune is more sensitive because she's Black."

That got Jason's attention. "Exactly what are you insinuating?"

"Nothing! All I'm saying is that maybe she is hearing something more than what is there, and it's causing you to see Seth's words as harsher than what they really are. She probably has to be on guard all the time."

Graham's expression was so blank, Jason wondered if Graham believed the crap he was saying.

Graham continued, "Look. Seth is not a positive dude. He's always been a little on the angry side. That's just the way he is, which is why we call him the keg guy. Not because he brings the keg all the time, but because you need a keg's worth of beer around to dull some of his anger."

So, Jason hadn't been the only one who thought Seth's anger was more than what most people tolerated. Why this hadn't come out until now, though, was another mystery. Fortune wasn't "hearing something more", but Graham was right about Seth's anger—it was hard to handle.

Ranjan snorted dismissively as if the whole conversation were a pile of horse manure.

"Well, you got something to say? Just say it," Jason challenged him.

"I will. Fortune's right. Seth's a racist ass. He's always been that way. And from what you said, his stripes are showing."

Graham and Jason gaped at Ranjan.

"How long have you known this?" Graham asked.

Ranjan laughed. "Are you kidding me? Have you even heard some of the jokes he makes?"

"Why are you just now saying something about it?"

He shrugged. "Seth's your friend. I wasn't going to be the home wrecker, especially when none of it was directed at me. When he'd get to be too much, I'd leave."

Jason thought back to the times when Ranjan would disappear. He thought it was because Ranjan had a boyfriend he wanted to keep secret. He never considered Seth being the reason for the disappearances. And there had been a lot over the years. Even in college.

Jason wracked his brain to conjure memories of Seth's conversations during those times, but nothing came to him. "How did we miss this?" he asked under his breath.

"We weren't looking for it," Graham responded, shocking Jason that he was heard over the bar's noise. "The question is what do we do about it now?"

"The only thing to do. Go to Seth and figure out what his deal is." Jason sighed. "I'll let you know how it goes." He turned to leave.

"Wait! You're going now? Shouldn't we all do this together?" Graham said.

"I'm the one who started this whole group date thing. If he's got beef with anyone, it's me. Thanks for the beer and the feedback."

"The dates were kind of fun. I quite liked them," Ranjan said.

Jason realized he'd thought the dates were fun, too. Instead of leaving, he asked the server for a glass of water and turned back to his friends.

After a couple of glasses of water to sober up and some more time chatting with his friends, Jason left The Graveyard and called Seth. Why he decided to call instead of going with the whole gang for a proper discussion was a mystery that he should've solved before he'd placed the call. He just knew this was something he'd have to do alone. He needed to get to the bottom of this and find a solution. Besides, Jason was the one who fixed things, not Graham or Ranjan.

Instead, he'd opened a Pandora's box and unleashed chaos.

Seth's voice crackled through Jason's car speaker, the telltale sign that both were on the road. "You sound like you're driving. Still doing late nights at the office?"

"Nah, I'm coming from Tina's house."

"You're seeing a lot of her lately."

Jason hadn't even asked about the group dates, but Seth weighed in on them immediately. "You should stop doing these group date things forever. They're a waste of time and money."

Jeez, the guy was already on the offensive with one simple question. Jason wondered if Tina had broken up with Seth and kicked him out. She needed to let him go, for nothing else but her safety. Jason thought back to what she'd said about Seth's angry outburst after the movie date. He could do much worse if he were fired up after a confrontation. Jason needed to warn her after he and Seth had their conversation in case they were still together.

"What's going on, man?" Seth's voice burst through the crackle.

Jason took a deep breath, still wondering why he needed to broach this with Seth at this moment. The truth would probably be best, Jason thought. Maybe not all the truth like Ranjan's confessions, but some of it would at least help fix things. *Here I go fixing things again.*

But Jason found that for the first time ever, he had nothing to say to Seth. *I should have waited for the guys, but no. I had to confront this right now.* Jason wondered if he disconnected the call would Seth try to call back or just give up.

"You know Fortune said the same thing about the group dates."

"Well, at least we agree on something."

"I think you'll find you agree on more than that."

Seth's laugh sounded like a witch's cackle through the speaker. "Unlikely."

Jason sighed. "How about we meet and talk about this next week before making any decisions? You free Tuesday? We can meet at Johnny B's." Johnny B's was Seth's favorite bar hang, but Jason rarely went there. For one, it was on the other side of town. And two, he was never truly comfortable there; instead, he always felt like his back was against the wall and he would have to fight his way out of there at some point during the night.

Seth knew it, too. "You? At Johnny B's? Wow, you must either want something from me really badly, or pigs are competing with 747s for sky space."

Jason laughed, but a pang clanged against his ribcage.

Seth was already piecing things together and getting his defenses up. Well, no one said he wasn't smart. "Fine with me. It's your hill to die on."

What an awful phrase.

Nineteen

Jason

DRIVING TO JOHNNY B'S, Jason wondered why he cared so much about Seth's state of being. When the ladies had expressed their views, he thought the goal was to make Seth understand how his behavior affected others. After Jason's convos with the guys, he wasn't even sure why he was bothering talking to Seth at all. They had never been real buddies anyway, opting to fall in together only when they were all in a group.

Seth always joked that Graham and Jason were the ones in the bromance, and he was just the keg guy. It wasn't funny, but it was true—Seth always brought the drinks to any party they had, and Graham and Jason were closer friends because you couldn't talk to Seth about anything. He never took anything seriously, unless it was a grievance against him—then he wanted to call in the law, have the perpetrators arrested, tortured, then put to death. Talking to him was exhausting.

Graham was right about Seth bringing the keg; he needed to soften the blows of his overly harsh conversations.

Johnny B's was the dive-iest of dive bars. Unassuming from the outside, the inside walls were clad in rustic, wide-plank boards with license plates and random metal signs nailed to them. The tables and chairs were pub height and made with a combination of metal plumbing pipe and thick plywood painted in a high-gloss black. The bar extended across the entire back wall and had a dark-stained wood top and a tarnished sheet metal panel riveted to the front. It reminded Jason of the Boar's Nest, the bar Bo and Luke Duke frequented on the show *Dukes of Hazzard,* only ten times darker; it was seedy, filthy, and clannish. As soon as he entered, his arms erupted in gooseflesh, and he shivered with the chilly welcome, though the temperature was warmer than the outside breezy April day.

Seth was already there when Jason arrived. He was leaning against the bar in deep conversation with one of the bartenders, and from the looks of things, Seth had already had a few beers. His gaze was unfocused and soft, and there were three empty bottles lined up beside his arm; it was a trick he'd employed after college to keep count of how many he'd had. Jason wasn't sure if only three beers down was a good thing and maybe Seth would be a little more open to hearing what Jason had to say, or if it was a bad thing and Seth would be more combative and stubborn. It could go either way.

"An IPA, please," Jason told the bartender. "Whatever you have available."

The bartender sniffed and snarled as if to say *pretentious prick* but wordlessly retrieved a bottle from the cooler.

Jason handed the bartender a ten-dollar bill, and instead of handing him the change, the bartender put it in his tip jar.

Jason rolled his eyes. Yet another reason he hated this bar: everyone judged you by what type of drink you ordered. If someone ordered water with their beer, they were a lightweight. If they ordered an IPA or a craft beer, they were a hippie or a yuppie with money to burn. If they ordered anything flavored or fruity, they were a tourist that had been led to the wrong place. And if they ordered any brown liquor, they were either someone who could get you a job or a mob boss.

"You know better than to order that crap in here." Seth's speech was slower and louder than usual.

"And you know better than to drink more than half your body weight in alcohol in the middle of the day," Jason replied.

"Don't hate me because you aren't slim and beautiful." Seth made a flourish gesture in front of himself.

Jason laughed.

Seth said, "What's this meeting about, anyway? When are the rest of the guys coming?"

"Just us. I thought I mentioned that."

Seth scratched his head and shrugged. "Maybe you did. Guess I forgot."

Jason didn't waste time getting to the subject, the urge to get on with it and get out creeping over his skin. "What was going on with you at the movie Friday?"

"What do you mean?"

"You were like some rude, horny teenager. No one wanted to be seen with you. You even made Tina uncomfortable."

"What is it with you and Tina?" Seth brandished a superior grin. "You think you missed out, and now you're jealous?"

"No. I have my own girlfriend—"

Seth stopped grinning and rolled his eyes. "Oh, yeah, her."

Jason continued. "No one should feel uncomfortable with the person they're dating." He paused and let everything Seth wasn't saying sink in. Friday had really been about making Fortune uncomfortable enough that she wouldn't be welcome. Everyone else just got caught in the fray. Fortune's words came back to him: *sometimes relationships have to stay broken to function.* Surely, that didn't apply to their friendships.

But Fortune and Seth were not friends. In fact, Jason believed they were better defined as mortal enemies.

First things first. He had to figure out what was going on with Seth to get these group dates back on track. "You're not acting like yourself. Actually, you're acting too much like you. What's going on, man?"

"How can someone be 'too much' themselves? Anyway, nothing's going on."

"Bull."

Seth averted his gaze to the ceiling and took a heavy breath. His drunken state and overly exaggerated gestures made Jason think about villainous comic book characters. "You know that promotion I was supposed to get? I didn't. They gave it to some Black guy." He took a heavy swig of his beer. "I was a shoo-in, and he just came in with his dark skin and his white smile and took it."

Jason squinched his face. "What do dark skin and a white smile have to do with getting a promotion?"

"Maybe nothing. Maybe a whole heck of a lot. Some say it was affirmative action. And I believe 'em." Seth's words were slurring on the ends. "I mean this guy comes out of nowhere and gets this job? My job?"

Something uncomfortable and unfamiliar prickled in the back of Jason's throat. He'd only felt it a few times recently—when Fortune mentioned the term ABW, when Seth made the assumption about Black women at karaoke, and when he was surprised that Celeste's husband was both Black and Italian. "First of all, it wasn't your job. It was a promotion that was up for grabs. Second, affirmative action is supposed to be a step towards equality. You say this guy came from nowhere, right?"

"Yeah."

"What if he actually didn't come from nowhere? What if he had been working and proving himself for years to be promoted, only to be continually passed up by some white guy? How many people of color are even in management there?"

"Two. Three with him."

"Out of dozens of middle and senior management? Seth, that's crazy. If affirmative action did have a role to play, it was long overdue. And who's to say it did? Do you actually know that?"

"No one actually knows. Of course, the company would keep that from us so they can get their government kick-back."

"Now the company is against you, too? Why are you even working there, then?"

"I worked hard to get where I am! It was my time!"

"And you think you're the only one? Just because you think it's your time for a promotion, you think you should be granted one. That's privilege talking."

"See this?" Seth pointed and waved his droopy index finger in Jason's face. "This is that woman getting in your head. You're taking their side!"

"There are no sides! Black people are humans just like us."

"Blacks are nothing like us."

The unsettling prickle morphed into a full-bodied shudder. Jason couldn't believe his friend thought like this. He picked up one of Seth's empty bottles and waved it back in his face. "How many of these have you really had? Because you're talking crazy."

The bartender walked up and snatched the bottle from Jason and removed the others from the bar. "Your friend's had too many, but he's not far off. These foreigners are coming over here and taking our jobs and getting entitlements while we sit here and slave for a few dollars that they tax the heck out of, to have money for the entitlements."

Jason's eyes widened, and his jaw dropped.

The bartender furrowed his brow. "What?"

"I can't believe you just said that. Slaves don't make money. That's the definition of the term. And you're seriously going to refer to your blond, blue-eyed American self as a slave, when this guy's ancestors may really have been slaves?"

The bartender blinked.

"Now I know why I always feel uncomfortable every time I walk in here." He turned to Seth. "Look, I'm sorry you didn't get the promotion, but no matter who got it, the bottom line is none of us took it from you. Especially not Fortune. So, go work that out with your therapist or a punching bag or something. You're bringing the fun times down, man."

"You know what? I don't care what you do. I'm not going on another one of those. I'm done. They aren't going to make me see Fortune in a whole new way, which I know is why you started them. I don't see her differently. She's still a big, Black woman, and I don't like her."

Jason inhaled sharply. He'd been cursed out before, but he found the sting of Seth's words more painful than Jason had ever experienced. And Seth wasn't saying this about Jason but about Fortune. Somehow, that quadrupled the pain. He hurt for her, but he also hurt realizing that, after all his efforts, he might be unable to fix things.

He couldn't cut Seth out, but he had to give him some parameters. "I don't care if you don't like her. You're going to respect her."

"I don't have to respect anyone that doesn't respect me or my family!"

"What are you talking about?"

"The lady at the A&P back home that lured my dad away from our family, the girl that turned me down for homecoming and made me a laughingstock, Fortune always trying to make me look bad every chance she gets. Black women are nothing but trouble. They don't deserve my respect!" He blew out a breath like a bull spotting a matador unfurling his cape. His scowling face and neck dotted with bright red spots, and his eyes, which were hazy and unfocused before were now sharp and trained on Jason.

He was stymied for words. Even though Seth was disgruntled most of the time, Jason had never seen him this angry, especially when it came to women. Usually, he was almost dismissive when it came to women. Most of all, he'd never talked about his past with the guys. The most Jason knew was that Seth's parents were divorced and lived in Jacksonville, Florida. Hatred had to come from somewhere; Seth's came from his past hurt.

"Fortune's not making you look bad. You're doing that all on your own. Anyway, we're planning more group dates, so work this out of your system if you want to join us. You can't come around at the last minute and ruin a good time like you did at the movies."

"There's no working this out. You do what you want. I told you I'm done."

Jason's heart sank as he turned on his heel and left Johnny B's. He wasn't just walking away from an overpriced beer and two pretentious jerks, he was leaving decades of friendship. Walking into the bar, he'd thought by finding out what was eating Seth Grape, Jason would be well on the way to fixing things. Now, as he got in his car, he was resigned to the fact that he didn't have the tools to fix Seth, which meant that the whole group's dynamic was in jeopardy. All he did was tell Seth to fix himself, but it was clear he thought nothing was wrong.

Each day, Fortune's words kept coming back to bang him squarely in the forehead, knocking his vision clear of that friendship filter he'd been peering through since he'd met Seth. Her observations were like a dose of ipecac for an upset stomach—hard to swallow but necessary to feel better. He hated this.

Twenty

Jason

H E OPENED THE DOOR to an unsmiling Fortune. "Hey, sweetie." He leaned in to kiss her.

She offered him her cheek. "Hey, yourself. Thanks for letting me come by."

"Always. You don't have to ask."

She sat on the sofa and crossed her ankles. "Why are you friends with Seth?"

It was a simple question, but he was stymied for the answer. Suddenly, he felt like he had to make an excuse, and nothing he could say would be good enough. "We were the Eastcoasters."

"What? So, you're telling me all this time, you never noticed this racist in your friend group?"

Fortune's question clanged in his mind like an accusation. Inadequacy ate at him, while ignorance begged to defend him. Her voice was so even, and her expression was open, yet he still wanted to hide. He'd been avoiding this conversation since the crazy date night and ensuing fight at The Graveyard almost seven months ago. How had he not seen Seth's behavior until now? If he had, he would've addressed this before he'd found the love of his life, and they all would have gotten along.

"Jason? Are you listening?"

He'd been silent too long to make up an answer. Not that he would have with Fortune anyway; they'd done the hiding feelings thing already. "I noticed he was cynical and at times a jerk. I just didn't notice ..."

"That he was being a jerk to Black people? Or fat people? Or anyone who didn't look like him?"

"Ranjan doesn't look like him."

"Ranjan is friends with you and maybe Graham. Seth not so much. And I could see that from just a few encounters with him."

Jason sighed. "Our social circles aren't that wide."

Fortune sighed heavily. "But your privilege is. It allows you to be tolerant to haters and oblivious to hate."

Annoyance rose in Jason's gut. He hated that word "privilege", especially when it was being used as the reason for his behavior. But it blew off quickly as his ego forced him to let Fortune's words sink in. She was right. He never needed to conform or check any of his friends, mostly because he'd lived a pretty white life in what he now saw as a pretty white society. Now that he had a Black girlfriend, he'd have to take the blinders off and get a clue.

Fortune tugged his left bicep with both hands to get his attention. "You can't fix this. So, you're going to have to decide between him and me."

Jason looked into her eyes. The decision was easy, but there had to be a solution for what to do about Seth. "It's you, of course. I just need to figure out why Seth won't come around."

"Maybe there isn't a reason. Maybe it's how he was raised. Not everyone had inclusive parents like yours. Some model hatred or even teach their kids to hate, and a lot of times those kids can't unlearn it."

If that was the case, how could he fix things?

"Or maybe he was wronged by someone. Maybe a Black woman stepped on his heart and crushed it. Maybe his boss is a Black woman, and she's a bad boss. I don't know. But I also don't care. I'm not any of those people. So, I'm not going to entertain his excuses because I've done nothing to him." She took a sip of wine then nestled back into the sofa.

"I would not expect you to."

"We're just not going to get along, and I don't want to be around him. So, you're going to have to choose. There's no fixing us; we aren't going to be friends."

Fortune

Shadows fell over Jason's face as the first floor got darker. Day had become night while they sat in his living room working through how to deal with Seth. "He's been hurt, and

I think he's internalizing it. Apparently, he lost a promotion at work. They gave it to a ... Black guy." Jason inhaled sharply.

Fortune scrunched her face and looked up at the ceiling for a moment, forcing what he said to make sense with what she understood. "I get it. It must be upsetting to see someone you love loving people who hated you or hurt you. People who hurt you for the same reason they could harm the one you loved. He probably sees you the same way. How could you be with a Black woman when another Black person had taken something he thought was his? And took it supposedly because the guy was Black?

"But thinking a promotion was his and someone actually saying 'We're giving this promotion to this guy because he's Black' are two different things."

And it didn't change the fact that Fortune had more than proven herself by welcoming Seth and being as friendly as possible. And all Seth had done was make his friends uncomfortable and pit them against each other. He was willing to destroy over two decades of friendship because he couldn't stop being a racist. Her heart burned in anger, but tears spilled from her eyes. If she hadn't met Jason and fallen so deeply in love, none of this would be happening.

She was so heavy with frustration and grief that she was sure she'd sunk inches deep in the ground. "I get it, Jason. I really do. But it doesn't explain Seth's behavior before all of this. Has he been competing with this guy ever since Seth saw me at Silver Foxes? It's more than just a promotion."

"Sweetie, maybe we're rushing this. You're not giving him enough time to come around. To get over this setback."

Whoa. Fortune got up and walked toward the opposite side of the room to put some distance between them.

"No. Don't put this on me. I am not the problem!" She shook her head, rubbing the spot between her scrunched-together eyebrows and holding back more tears. She was not going to cry any more over this guy. "Your 'friend' is the problem!"

Jason stared hard at her, forcing his feet to stay put. "You're going to make me choose between my girlfriend and my friend of over twenty years?"

She'd known this day was coming. They'd tiptoed around it for weeks, but they couldn't anymore. Jason finally understood he would have to sacrifice something, or it all would implode in hurt and misery. Still, why was he asking her as if *she* were the reason he would have to make a choice? "Are you really asking me that? You realize I'm your girlfriend, right? The one you're talking to?"

"Maybe if I could get him to see that it's more than group dates ..."

She paced the walkway between the kitchen island and the living room like she was racing, her steps so hard they made clomping noises across his hardwood floors. "You don't think he knows that? You keep trying with him, and I'm telling you not to. Don't do this to us. You're going to break us up! You're going to do this to us? Why?"

"Fortune! Stop!" In seconds, he closed the distance between them. He grabbed her arm.

She yanked it free of his grasp. "I ... I can't be around this anymore. I can't be ... infected by this. Racism is a virus,

you know. It doesn't just hang out in one area of your life
and infect that. It takes over everything—your thoughts,
your vision, your beliefs, and then it's on to the next person
you infect until all of you are wiped out, overtaken with
the illness. I will not watch you get infected. I've got to go.
Goodbye."

Jason

His group date plan was a failed mistake. He was supposed
to be Mr. Fix-it. Instead, he was breaking everything—his
relationship with Fortune, his friends, and even his own
happiness was taking a sound beating. How had this happened?

Sometimes, no matter what you do or show people, they
aren't going to change. People can only be who they are and
who they become.

That's what'd happened with Seth. He hadn't changed,
but slowly, they had. They'd unconsciously adapted themselves to tolerate him. He'd have to end things with the
group dates and with Seth. It was the only fix he had left.

Jason invited Seth to Beans & Bread for a cup of decaf
and a chat. When Jason arrived, Seth was already seated,
nursing a mug of something steaming, the condensation
from it forming water droplets against his forehead.

Seth looked up as if he sensed his friend and nodded
Jason's way.

Seth looked the same as always, but now under this new light of understanding, he was a stranger. The creases in his forehead deepened when he talked about losing a promotion to "this Black guy" he worked with. The malicious stare in his eyes flared when he made sexual comments about a Latina personal trainer at the gym where they were members. The vein in his temple popped when Fortune said something witty. And as much as Tina's antics annoyed Jason, they barely registered with Seth. Was it because she was Tina? Or was it because she was white?

As Jason stood in line to order and wait for his coffee, he thought about how to handle Seth. But what about the rest of his friends? Would he end up alone because he failed at bringing them together?

Jason made his way to Seth's table. "Thanks for meeting with me. We need to talk."

"So, you're breaking up with me instead of her."

"What are you talking about?" Jason quirked his lips into a confused frown.

"'We need to talk?' Total breakup line. Why you would choose her over me, though, I'll never understand. The sex can't be that good with all that extra weight to get around."

A surge of adrenaline shot through Jason, and his fingers curled into fists.

Calm down, Reed. He can't talk if his lip is busted.

"That's not why I asked you here, and I definitely didn't ask you here for you to crack jokes at my girlfriend's expense, so lay off."

Seth raised both hands in surrender.

Jason snarled. "Listen, we've been friends a long time, supported each other through a lot of good decisions and bad. I'm asking you to put aside whatever animosity you have towards Fortune so we can all continue to be friends here. She's going to be around a while."

"Yeah, I don't think so. Dude, she just doesn't fit in. As soon as she realizes that, she's out of here."

"She fits in as my girlfriend, and that's the only way that matters. I love her. In fact, I plan to propose to her." Jason pulled a small navy-blue velvet box out of his pants pocket. He'd wanted Graham to be the first friend to see it, but he needed Seth to understand how important Fortune was. And that she'd be in their lives permanently. "Picked it up from the jeweler's on the way here."

Seth leaned back in his chair and crossed his arms. "No." He stared into space, shaking his head. "No, no, no, man. Don't mess up your life like this."

The animosity vibrating off Seth was enough to shake Beans & Bread off its foundation, as if Jason's words were a match and Seth was a stick of dynamite ready to explode. Why was he *this* angry? Couldn't Seth see how close he and Fortune were? None of Seth's reactions made sense. If he was truly a friend, he would have been happy for Jason no matter what.

"Why don't you like her?" Jason asked. "Is it because she knee'd you at Silver Fox? Dude, you gotta get over that. You were a jackass, and she had every right to do that."

"You weren't the one who got a knee in the 'nads. But no, that isn't why."

"Well, what is it?"

"She ... I ..." He sighed with frustration. "She wears tank tops, okay?"

"What?"

"She shouldn't be allowed to wear those in public. Have you even noticed her arms?"

Jason guffawed. "You're causing a rift in the group because you don't like my girlfriend's arms?"

Seth seethed. "It's more than that, but that's part of it. She's not ashamed of her size. No one wants to see all of that ... brown skin."

He was getting antsy. "Watch it, Seth. That's my woman you're talking about." He shook his head. "Fortune was right. Again. You really are racist and fat phobic, and no matter what I do or say, you're not going to change. Why have I never seen this?" The revelation came to him as he spoke, almost like looking at how a sunrise slowly brightens everything it touches.

"You're going to regret this. Everyone I know who's hooked up with one of them regrets it. It's not going to last!"

"What the hell? I don't know what to say to that." Jason rose to leave, but Seth seized his forearm, stopping him.

"Listen, in high school, I asked this Black girl out to homecoming junior year. We were chemistry lab partners, then we became friends. We even hung out after school, waiting for the late bus to pick us up. I liked her. I really liked her."

For a moment, his eyes softened with wistfulness. "And I thought she liked me. So, when I asked her to the dance, I was sure she'd say yes, but she didn't. Turned me down between third and fourth period, claiming she didn't think of me like that, and she was going with someone else anyway. By lunch, all my so-called friends had heard what happened. I never lived that down."

Jason's eyes widened in surprise, then briefly closed in sorrow. "I'm not going to stop loving Fortune because you had a bad experience with a Black woman."

"You've never dated anyone like this! Fat *and* Black! What are you, some humanitarian organization?"

A surge of heat burned in Jason's chest. "We're done." He got up from the table.

"Seriously, Jas—"

He turned and glared at his now former friend. Fortune said he wasn't going to be able to fix their friendship; he would have to choose instead—Fortune or Seth. And Jason wasn't giving up on the love of his life. He clutched the ring box inside his pocket. "No. You don't get to talk about my girlfriend that way, and we remain cool. We. Are. Done. I'm going to leave now, so I don't knock you the hell out."

After Jason exited, he thought about what Seth had said. On one point, Seth was right: Jason had never dated someone like Fortune. Maybe that was why he hadn't been truly happy until now.

Maybe that was why he almost married a closeted woman. He hadn't seen real beauty until Fortune because he was caught up in what everyone else said was beautiful. Lesson learned. He'd never trust his search for happiness to anyone but himself and his instincts.

Twenty-One

Fortune

AFTER GIVING JASON AN ultimatum, she shouldn't have been in Beans & Bread trying to find him, but here she was peering around the coffee shop and chiding herself as she did. Her eyes burned and blurred with tears and tiredness.

Fortune spotted Seth as he walked her way. Ugh. The last person she wanted to see. But maybe he knew where Jason was. "Hi, Seth. Have you seen Jason?"

"You actually just missed him. I think he was headed home. Or over to Tina's. I'm not sure."

She eyed him curiously. "And you're okay with that?"

He chuckled. "Why wouldn't I be? Tina and I aren't together. I mean, we've hung out a few times, but we're not really right for each other. Now Tina and Jason, those two should stop dancing around it and hook up already."

Fortune frowned. "Your point, Seth?" she asked over her shoulder as she made her way to the counter.

"I don't have a point. He probably just went home." He sounded almost giddy. "But why are you looking for him? I thought you were broken up."

She whipped around to face him. "Who told you that?"

He smiled. Actually smiled! "He told me when he was in here. He said he had to break up with you because you gave him some kind of ultimatum."

Fortune closed her eyes for a brief second as a wave of nausea went through her. Talking to Seth was making her ill. No way had Jason picked him over her, even if they were fighting. He was lying to force her into being the ABW he probably thought she was.

She wasn't going to take the bait. Fortune turned to the cashier and ordered to keep the line moving. "I told him it was either me or you. Guess he picked you," she said, her back still to him, her voice as unwavering as possible.

"You know we should go and talk to him together," Seth suggested. "Just because we don't see eye to eye right now, doesn't mean you two have to part ways."

"I was planning to go over to talk to him." She picked up the decaf latte and cinnamon roll she ordered.

"Good. Then it's decided." He followed her out the door.

What drugs had Seth been taking? It had to have been some powerful stuff for him to be nice to her and want to work things out among the three of them. Nope. She wasn't going to believe this until she experienced it. She headed to her car.

"Why don't we take my car since he's just around the corner?" Seth suggested. "No need to clog up all the parking spaces in front of Jason's building."

He wasn't a stranger, but all of a sudden, her brain screamed "stranger danger" so loudly it was almost audible. She envisioned an unflattering photo of her face on the news with the word "missing" stamped across the front. There were silver alerts for older people and amber alerts for children, but what about forty-year-old Black women?

There's nothing. No one cares if we go missing except us.

Instead of taking Seth up on his offer, she opened her own car door. "I'd rather take my own car."

Seth came around to meet her. "Why?"

"Really, Seth? You called me a whale, then almost called me a big Black bitch. You've either sabotaged every group date Jason planned or you just disappeared, and now you want to go to his house with me in some manufactured kumbaya moment? I'm not falling for that."

"I'm trying to be on your side here, and you want to turn that against me? What's with you people?"

"'You people', huh?" She leaned inside her car and set down her Beans & Bread purchase. Her mind was racing, calculating how to diffuse what could become a volatile situation with the least stimulus. The call button on her steering wheel. She slid her hand to it while turning back to Seth, praying that what she was thinking would work. "You know this is becoming a little heated. Maybe we should—" She pressed the button "call Jason before we go by his place.

That should give us some time to cool off and think things over."

When she heard the click of Jason answering, Fortune turned the volume down to barely intelligible. She heard him saying, "Fortune? You there?"

In response to Seth, she said, "He'd probably appreciate a call first. We could tell him that we met up here at Beans & Bread, and since we were so close, we decided to stop by."

Jason was saying something she couldn't make out. Afraid Seth would hear, she turned the volume off completely.

But Seth wasn't cooling down. Instead, he scrunched his shoulders, narrowed his eyes, and snarled. "What is with you always dictating? You're always giving orders like somebody's mama."

"That's not what I was trying to do."

"Where are you from anyway?"

The question caught Fortune off-guard for a few seconds, but she quickly saw it for the microaggression it was. This had gone on long enough. "I'm from Nebraska. And I've grown up with people like you. So, if you're trying to scare me away from Jason, don't bother. It's a futile effort. But if you want to iron out our differences and get to a place where we can both be in his life, then I'm all for it."

"You're not meant to be together. It's just not natural."

Here we go with this.

What year was it again? You'd think by the twenty–first century, people would have figured out we're all humans. No such luck here. "You have no right—"

"He can't marry you."

What was this guy talking about? "What?"

"Just because he bought a ring doesn't mean he should marry you."

Jason bought a ring? They had talked about rings, but she assumed all of that was on hold after the fight between them.

Jason was choosing her after all.

And Seth was livid. "You're the reason he's all messed up. His priorities are screwed up because of you."

She glanced up at him and received a hate-filled stare that felt like porcupine needles in her face. She suddenly registered the change in the energy from him, going from a twinge of jealousy to full-on violent hatred.

And she was alone in a parking lot, without the baseball bat her dad had given her to defend herself. She thought it was a joke when he'd given it to her as a housewarming gift, but now she wished it was in her hands instead of her coat closet collecting dust.

Seth closed the distance between them in seconds, pinned her against the back door of the car, and seized her throat with both hands.

Twenty-Two

Jason

J ASON SAT IN HIS parking space for what seemed like hours, listening to mellow Emo music on 106.5 and feeling defeated. Seth wasn't going to come around. Every moment Jason observed, every snide remark he'd heard, and every tactless joke he'd cringed at from Seth since the group dates started led him to two conclusions: Seth had been hurt when he hadn't gotten the promotion, but he was also a racist.

Racist.

The word permeated Jason's thoughts making him feel as sick as riding a roller coaster on a full stomach of greasy fair food. He breathed deeply and covered his face with his hands. Relief and finality buoyed him as he walked out of Beans & Bread, but now, he was awash in disbelief and hurt.

He'd been friends with a racist.

His head pounded, so he squeezed his eyes shut and pressed the pads of his fingers into his forehead. It didn't relieve the throbbing. Maybe nothing would. Being cursed with a perpetual headache until the end of time sounded like the right amount of punishment for befriending a racist.

The group hadn't been *woke* or whatever the kids said now. They hadn't even been paying attention. He and his friends had just passed off Seth's behavior as a personality trait, never questioning why he was a basic jerk or even hearing what he was actually saying. And because everyone got the blunt end of Seth's attitude once in a while—Graham and Jason were no exception—no one even thought he was being a racist. Seth was just a jerk, plain and simple. Or so they believed. If he hadn't met Fortune, they all would've still been in the dark, obliviously indulging "the keg guy" in the name of friendship.

Fortune didn't just light up a room, she enlightened his life. He couldn't lose her, especially for this dude. As a vision of Fortune's bright smile formed in his mind, the phone rang.

She was already mid-conversation before he could even say hello. "Fortune?" She was rambling something about Beans & Bread, but he couldn't make it out. "Fortune? You there?"

She wasn't talking to him. It had probably been a butt dial. He should just hang up.

And then he heard Seth's voice. His tone was controlled, but he was clearly angry.

What was going on?

Raised voices from them both. Shuffling. And then a loud thump and a high-pitched yelp that was cut short.

Was he? Couldn't be.

Rage shook Jason like a high wind on a tree branch.

If he hurts her, I will kill him.

He hopped out of the car, ready to run to Beans & Bread and destroy his former friend, but stopped when he heard Seth say, "What are you doing to him?" He couldn't hear Fortune's response. He couldn't hear Fortune at all.

Twenty-Three

Fortune

ALARM SEIZED EVERY NERVE and electrified her as if she'd touched a live wire.

Panic shook her.

She fought it, urging her body to calm.

Didn't work.

She shook like a leaf, her dangly earrings clinking against each other.

Was this a cruel joke?

She couldn't reconcile what was going on with reality.

Seth's grizzly voice sounded unnatural. "What are you doing to him? Is it because of the crap you're telling him?" Leaving one hand against her throat, with the other, he groped her from her neck down her body and then jammed a hand between her legs. "Or maybe it's this?"

Fear and adrenaline instantly flooded her body.

Her mind raced with thoughts, but she couldn't focus on anything except his hands. The hand around her neck was smooth and cold and crushing, like a piece of heavy steel. The one between her legs was uncomfortable to the point of pain. His hands felt like humiliation wrapped in death.

Her heart hammered through her chest.

Her legs wanted to run, but she couldn't.

Fear paralyzed her.

Her eyes widened as he tightened his grip on her throat with one hand and, with the other, pushed the fabric of her underwear and capri pants almost inside her.

She was trapped.

Her throat was burning from his grip, preventing her from screaming. She could only make whimpering, shallow breaths. Tears stung her eyes then coursed down her cheeks.

No. You can't let him see you cry. You can't give him that power.

Instead, she took in the parking lot, half-shadowed in darkness, searching for something to focus on that would keep her from crying.

His voice came out in a grisly rasp that caused her stomach to clench. "We don't want you here. Go back to that ghetto you came from."

Standing on legs the consistency of jelly, Fortune struggled to ignore his taunts and locked her attention instead to a cluster of lights in the distance. They became less like lights and more like bright spots.

She weakly whined and squirmed.

He effortlessly leaned his full weight against her.

Her heart thudded wildly.

Her face was hot with effort and frustration. Breathing was hard. The lights ... were fading.

Twenty-Four

Jason

HIS RATIONAL SIDE FORCED him to ratchet down his anger enough to disconnect Fortune's call and dial 911 instead. Then he got back behind the wheel and rushed to his favorite coffeehouse, hoping he was overreacting.

He wasn't.

At the sight of Fortune pinned against her car with Seth's hands on her, adrenaline ripped through Jason with lighting heat.

He jumped out of the car and moved fast and with precision.

Jason's voice reverberated into the parking lot over the muffled sounds of struggle. "What the hell are you doing?"

He shoved Seth off her. "Keep your hands off my wife!"

He pushed Seth until the man was off Fortune and on the ground.

But before Jason could get to her, Seth was back up and retaliating.

Jason punched Seth in the ribs, followed by another to the gut.

Seth wheezed, then swung blindly.

Jason ducked and blocked a few more of Seth's blows.

Seth kicked Jason in the chest hard.

Jason fell back on the passenger side of Fortune's car and dropped to his knees, his breath gone.

When Seth leaned in to assess the damage, Jason punched up and hit him in the face. His hand stung as it connected with Seth's jaw.

Seth screamed a curse.

Now that he'd gotten his wind back, Jason hopped up.

Blue, white, and red flashing lights illuminated the night as police and rescue teams came to an abrupt halt in the tiny parking lot. Sirens drowned out the grunts and thumps of Jason and Seth pummeling each other. The lot went from lonely and isolated to active and crowded in seconds.

"Freeze! Hands up. Freeze!" Police officers advanced on them, their flashlights almost blinding Jason.

He held up his hands, but he couldn't keep still, frantically searching for Fortune. He spotted her at the same time Seth threw a punch. "Help her! Help my girlfriend! This jerk assaulted her."

He subdued Seth for the officers and then raced to Fortune, struggling to stand despite the paramedics telling her to stay seated.

"Fortune? Sweetie?"

Twenty-Five

Fortune

W HILE SETH AND JASON fought, Fortune collapsed against the car and then sank to the ground in a heap. The world was a quiet, dark hole. She heard punches landing and saw shadows moving, but nothing was in focus.

Thank God that calling stunt worked.

Fortune gritted her teeth in frustration and anger, her fear keeping her immobile as Seth and Jason traded jabs. She should have been fighting back. Why didn't she? She couldn't even move.

She could have kicked herself.

Thank goodness Jason was there.

Wait a minute. Did he call her his wife?

No time to focus on that now.

She shook her head, but that emphasized her sore neck and the rawness in her throat. She grasped her throat to protect it and attempted to get up.

She caught her breath, crawled to the grassy curb, and sat down, elbows on knees.

Sudden daylight blinded her. No, not daylight.

"Freeze! Hands up. Freeze!" Two police officers emerged surefooted but slowly, brandishing firearms.

Fortune sat frozen, hands in the air, but after Jason's plea, the police officers left Fortune to the paramedics and advanced to Jason.

The female officer cuffed Seth while the other held Jason. "Ma'am, is what he's saying true?"

"Yeah, that's my boyfriend." The rough, cracked sound of Fortune's voice surprised her. Seth's attack was evident. Still, she couldn't have been that badly hurt. She pushed against the curb to give herself momentum to stand.

The paramedic reached for her. "Ma'am? Don't get up yet. Let us help you."

"Too slow," Fortune mumbled. The effort made her dizzy, and she slumped back to the pavement.

Jason broke away from the officer's hold and rushed towards her, bending and thrusting out his arms to help. "Wait, let me—"

"I've got it. I've got it!" She waved him off while lurching to her feet. After all, she hadn't been punched or thrown against anything. Just a little wind knocked out of her when Seth had... She shook her head, unable to even think about what he'd done.

All of a sudden, things blurred around her. Jason's hands morphed into cream-colored blobs dancing in front of her eyes.

"Forrrrtuunne? Sweetieee?" His words were like cold molasses trickling down the side of a jar.

The paramedic was calling her. "Missss ...?"

She wanted to respond. She really did. Something heavy and paralyzing was taking over her.

"Oh, no!"

Everything went black.

Twenty-Six

Jason

THE STRONG, VIBRANT WOMAN he loved fell into his arms in a dead faint. At least, that's what he hoped had happened. He braced her with one arm and cradled her face with his other hand, hoping his touch would wake her. "Fortune!"

She made no movement outside the miniscule rise and fall of her chest.

He patted her cheek. "Sweetie? Can you hear me?"

She didn't respond.

His insides constricted.

One of the EMTs touched his shoulder. "Sir, let us help her."

He didn't want to let her go, arguing with the paramedics about taking her to the emergency room, but eventually, he relented when they said she could have a concussion or take a turn for the worse.

The other paramedic separated them so they could work. He sat there, stunned, until they got her on a stretcher.

An EMT went to him. "Sir? She's going to be fine. You can follow us. No lights, okay? She's going to be alright."

"Yeah. Yes, sure. Sure, I can." Jason shook out of his haze and sprang into action. He gathered Fortune's belongings from the fiasco and hopped into her car. As the doors of the back of the ambulance closed on the unconscious love of his life, he shook his head but failed to shake away the vision of her body falling into his arms.

What could be worse than that?

Riding behind the ambulance to the hospital gave him more than enough time to think and to chastise himself. Seeing her lying there in the bright light of the vehicle's interior, with a paramedic hovering over her, fueled the anger and guilt raging in him. Seth was a hateful jerk, but assault? No. As long as Jason knew him, he'd never been violent. Or at least Jason thought he hadn't. What did he really know about Seth? One thing Jason was becoming increasingly aware of was that, as surely as the sky was blue, he wanted to kill Seth.

The ambulance pulled into the emergency bay.

Jason swerved into the first available parking space and hopped out, meeting the paramedics as they wheeled in Fortune.

He matched the pace of the paramedics into the emergency room and grabbed Fortune's hand. "Sweetie, It's Jason. Can you hear me?"

One paramedic interrupted. "Sir, she's still unconscious. Let's get her admitted."

The other paramedic walked beside him. She had a lighter tone and smiled amiably. "The best thing you can do now is wait for her in the lobby."

Jason let go of Fortune's hand and stepped back. "Please take care of her."

"We will. I promise."

Jason headed out to the emergency lobby, phone in hand.

Graham answered with a smug tone. "Hey, man. Ready for another *Madden* smack-down?"

When Jason gave him a quick run-down of the night's events, Graham went from smug to serious. "Sounds like you have the hospital thing down, and they'll probably release her soon. I'll call Ranjan, and we'll meet you at Fortune's house. Text me the address."

"Yeah. Okay."

"She's going to be fine, Jase."

Graham only used the nickname when he could tell Jason was stressed. And the whole time, he'd been thinking, *be calm*. Guess that hadn't come across. "Yeah, I am. I mean, I know."

Twenty-Seven

Fortune

B RIGHT LIGHTS. THE WARMTH of the lights hitting her eyelids eased them open. Was she still in the parking lot? No. These were different bright lights.

Fortune opened her eyes to several masked faces of strange people hovering over her. They were crowding her, blocking out the light. But they were too close. Too many of them. Too close.

"Ms. Edwards? Do you know where you are?" one face said.

"Ms. Edwards? Could you stretch out your arm for me?" another face said.

Fortune's heart beat at a breakneck pace, and she felt it in her throat.

Stay away from me.

She fought the urge to push the faces away from her, but the urge was winning.

"Ms. Edwards, you're okay. You're at University Memorial Hospital," the first face said.

If I'm at a hospital, I'm not okay.

Another face crowded out even more of the light. "Can you tell us what happened?"

Enough.

Fortune writhed and screamed. "Get off me! Go away!" It came out hoarse and scratchy. Her throat felt like it was on fire.

The faces started talking frantically at once. She couldn't make out what they were saying. She just knew she had to get away. They had to go away.

"Noooooo!" she wailed.

She was back in the parking lot, struggling in Seth's grimy clutches as he tried to squeeze the life out of her. She wasn't going to stand by and let him win. She was fighting back.

"Not this time! No!" She fought the faces and arms coming for her until she felt her body slowing. It was like someone was blanketing her insides. She was losing. Again.

"No ... Not again," she whimpered.

The light was getting dimmer. And then everything was black again.

Twenty-Eight

Jason

THE HOSPITAL STAY WAS the longest—he checked his watch—three hours of his life. "Can someone tell me how Fortune Edwards is doing?" he pleaded with the ER intake team.

"Sir, if you could just have a seat, we'll be right with you." The receptionist waved her hand over the half-full waiting room.

"Are you her emergency contact?" A man in scrubs with a shock of gray hair cut into a mohawk walked up to the counter and interrupted the exchange.

"Yes," he answered without hesitation, knowing it wasn't true. Her mother was probably her emergency contact. Dammit. He was going to have to explain this whole night to her mother. They should probably just wheel him away, instead of entrusting him with Fortune.

"Follow me." The ER doctor rattled off her symptoms, her condition when she'd been brought in, and recommendations as if he were reading a recipe for the most ingredient-heavy dish in culinary history. Jason pulled what he could from it and retained that for later, when surely it would come back up. Thankfully, there were no concussions or any other major internal damage. Her mental and emotional states were the real problems. She'd awoken shortly after arriving, and immediately after seeing everyone around her, she yelled incoherently and cried. A couple of nurses tried calming her but couldn't. So, the doctor prescribed Valium.

They approached the bay where Fortune lay, nothing like the banshee the doctor described. Apparently, the Valium had kicked in. He scribbled out a prescription for more and handed it to Jason. "Make sure she takes this with water, no more than twice a day. I've only given her three days' worth. More than anything, she'll need someone to talk to. A licensed therapist. Somebody other than you. You're Mister Edwards, I take it?"

No. "Yes."

"Then definitely not you. The anger is coming off you in waves. You'll need your own therapist."

He stared at the doctor blankly. What was this guy saying? He wasn't the one who was hurt. Fortune was.

"Anyway, we're done here."

Jason rushed to Fortune's side while an ER nurse helped her into a wheelchair. "Sweetie, let's go home."

Fortune peered up at him under half-closed eyelids. "Sure thing, Mister Edwards."

"You heard that, huh?"

"Yep. Has a nice ring to it."

"And Mrs. Reed doesn't?" Jason raised an eyebrow.

"Isn't that your mother?"

He left her side for only a moment when he got the car and pulled it to the emergency room's doorway.

Fortune settled in the passenger seat. "This is my car. I don't remember coming here in my car."

"You didn't. You came here in an ambulance." Jason's spine tensed as he slid into the driver's seat. He didn't want her to remember too much too fast. If she went into a freak-out the way she had in the emergency room, he wouldn't know what to do. But her drooping eyelids assured him that she probably wasn't connecting what he was saying to what had happened.

"Well, thanks for getting my car. And me. Thanks for supporting me ..." She slumped into a Valium-induced stupor.

If he *had* supported her before and chosen her over Seth, he wouldn't be taking her home from the hospital now. There was no way she'd agree to being Mrs. Reed after all this.

Twenty-Nine

Fortune

THEY LEFT A HOSPITAL emergency room she couldn't remember being in—or arriving at—and Jason ushered her into the passenger seat of her own car like an invalid. To be fair, she was definitely on some strong drugs that apparently erased panic, fear, and even sadness. She remembered joking with Jason about last names and ... parents?—she couldn't recall exactly—as they left. But nothing was all better. The mood in the car was tense and heavy. The angry vibes coming from Jason hit her like a strong whiff of bad perfume—off-putting. She recoiled.

Jason hadn't just pushed Seth. They'd fought—Jason had the cuts and bruises to prove it, but Fortune thought that had diffused things. Seth had been hauled into the back of a police car, and Jason had been cooling off in the ER. Surely, he'd calmed down by now. He'd even made a mild joke as they went to the car. But when Fortune spotted Graham and

Ranjan in her driveway, she knew that Jason wasn't okay. In fact, he was far from it if he had called them.

The expressions on Graham's and Ranjan's faces confirmed her suspicions. They exchanged glances with Jason and then with each other, worried brows and concerned pursed lips. If Fortune was unsure if Jason was still angry, his friends' expressions told everything. He was not over it. She guessed that was probably normal; after all, she wasn't over it either. Then again, she was the victim.

"Hi, guys." Fortune hoped her tone conveyed more cheer than she felt.

Honestly, she had no idea what her emotions were doing. A void resided inside where they should be. She was a walking shell of Fortune. She stumbled out of the car. A bruised, barely-walking shell, evidently.

Jason hurried to her side. "Sweetie, let me help. Where are your keys?"

He sounded so calm and sweet. But when he pressed her against his side, an uncomfortable heat radiated from his body, and his heart thudded so fast it vibrated in her. Fortune was glad that Ranjan and Graham were there. They'd seen a raging Jason and probably knew the best way to calm him.

"Fortune, are you feeling better?" Ranjan went to her other side and held her hand.

She smiled. "I'm fine. Turns out Valium makes everything fine."

"I'm sure it does."

Graham brought up the rear. "I'm sorry for what happened to you, Fortune."

Jason threw a stern glance over his shoulder.

Fortune caught a second of it and wondered what that was all about. "Thanks, Graham. But I'll be okay. Honest."

Ranjan rubbed his other hand across the back of hers. It was such a caring gesture, she wanted to cry. These guys knew her as well as a bump on a log, and they were showing they cared.

Jason opened the door, and they bustled inside. She wanted to snatch herself away from him with his heat and his hovering, but he was only trying to help. Still, he was too agitated, and she found it unnerving to be around him.

She asked him for a glass of water and made her way up the stairs to separate herself from him just for a moment. Maybe the guys would keep him downstairs and calm him down some.

Fortune peeled off her clothes and eased into the shower, relishing the first time she'd been alone since Beans & Bread. What had possessed her to even go over there? She'd given an ultimatum, and that should have been it. That's how it usually was with her relationships.

This time, she caved. Fortune had missed Jason. She went to the coffee shop with the hope that she would see him and they could work it out. Instead, she walked into a racist hell and couldn't leave with her body frozen under Seth's assault and her mind paralyzed with fear.

The numbness of the Valium was ebbing, and painfully sharp sadness took its place. Tears washed down her cheeks with the shower spray. "Why?" she moaned repeatedly to no one and crouched under the waterfall of water in a fetal position. The water beat against her back like a warm hug but did little to comfort her.

She never realized that she relied on her confidence as much as she had. She couldn't remember a time when she hadn't been strong and sure of herself. But now, as Fortune squatted broken and fragile in the warm shower, she realized she'd lost her confidence. It was gone—stolen when Seth violated her.

She banged her fists against her knees. "I can't live like this!"

Where had that confidence come from? It was more precious than any other resource on Earth. Fortune had to find out, so she could get it back.

"Sweetie? I got you a glass of orange juice, too, in case you needed something sweet." The bathroom door opened. "Fortune? Are you okay?"

Oh, yeah, here's where it is.

"No," she answered between sobs.

The shower curtain went back, and a blurry Jason stood there holding a towel. For a moment, he looked at her like he was afraid to touch her, but he quickly shook himself to action, turning off the shower, wrapping her in the towel, and ushering her out of the bathroom.

She stood sniffling as he dried her off and pulled a nightshirt over her head. She'd been violated. How could she move past this?

He folded back the covers and helped her into bed, then climbed in beside her, embracing her and pressing her to his chest. "It's going to be okay. I promise I won't let this happen again." He absently rubbed his palm up and down her arm, cuddled against her like a parent holding a sick child.

She always wondered why parents did that, knowing they could get sick, too, which they usually did.

Jason murmured soothing assurances into Fortune's hair, but his skin was still too hot and his heartbeat too fast to be calm.

So, she closed her eyes and lay still so he would think she had fallen asleep. She was still awake, despite the heavy drowsiness brought on by the Valium and the warm shower. But if he thought she found peace in sleep, maybe he could find peace, too. Anything to lower his agitation level—to take his mind off what had happened.

After a few moments, Jason shifted from around her and went into the bathroom, snicking the door closed behind him.

For a moment, it seemed the world had stopped.

A crash and a roar reverberated through the bathroom door.

Fortune gasped but didn't move, her heart skipping with anxiety. She heard a loud sniff and a sigh and then the whirl of water from the sink.

Her chest clenched, and tears welled in her eyes. For the first time ever, she felt helpless, unable to make Jason or the situation better. The rawness of her throat was minor compared to the stabbing ache deep in her soul at hearing him in pain. Jason was hurt because she had been hurt. And he was the one who could fix anything, not her.

Thirty

Jason

WHEN THEY ARRIVED AT Fortune's house, Ranjan and Graham were in Fortune's driveway leaning against Graham's car. The only light on was Fortune's side light, which barely cast a glimmer over the front of the car and shrouded his friends in shadows. Everything about this day was dark: seeing the darkness in Seth's heart manifest itself, feeling it when Jason had to say goodbye to his friend of more than twenty years, witnessing the terrifying dark moment when Fortune fainted.

Jason hurried to unlock the door and hustle Fortune inside before Graham could say another word. "Guys, can you excuse us? Babe, let me help you up the stairs."

"I've got it, Jason. Can you get me a glass of water, though? Make yourselves at home, guys."

There she was, doing too much again. He clenched his hands into fists.

Graham stepped up to him. "What is your problem, man?"

"She's hurting, and she won't let me help her."

"Dude, settle. She's trying to tell you she doesn't need help like that. The only way you can help her right now is by calming down and giving her some space."

Jason eased into her recliner sofa. "Yeah, I guess. The doctor did say she freaked out in the ER. Yelling about being suffocated or something. And she was already hoarse from where he ... choked her. She can barely talk now. If I could get my hands on him ... see how he likes being choked."

Graham took the seat beside him. "Knowing Seth, that's probably what he does for a good time."

Jason glared at his best friend again. "Graham—"

"I'm sorry. I heard it as I was saying it, and ... sorry."

Ranjan called from the kitchen. "Have you seen Fortune's beverage set-up? Espresso machine, fine teas, cute tea infusers, and themed mugs. This woman knows her way around a good hot beverage. I knew there was another reason I liked her."

Graham gave Jason a knowing look and smiled.

Jason's efforts at smiling back failed. "I'm going to go check on her." He jumped up and barreled into the kitchen, brushed past Ranjan, and poured a glass of water and a tumbler of orange juice. "I'll just be a minute, guys. Then, can you take me to get my car? I want to stay with her tonight."

"Sure, man," Graham said.

When Jason entered her room, he thought she would be in bed. Instead, he heard the shower running and a shaky humming sound just above it. Was she crying? It figured. She would want to put on a brave face in front of his friends. He'd seen her cry before, so maybe she would let him in.

"Fortune? Can I come in? Are you okay?"

A loud sniff. "No."

"I'm going to take that as *no* you're not okay, so I'm coming in."

When he pulled back the curtain, she was curled in the tub with the shower spray hitting her rounded spine. Disappointment and sadness hit him like a heavyweight champion's knockout blow, and he stood stunned.

Then anger built in his gut, and a heady swirl of emotions sprung him into action. He helped her out of the shower and into bed, avenging her by torturing and murdering Seth in his mind. It was an exaggeration, but his fury was real.

"He ..." Her voice hitched. "He grabbed me." She looked around the room as if the walls or the furniture had answers.

He wished they did so he could know them, too.

"He ... violated me." She dissolved into shaking sobs.

Jason rushed over and enveloped her in his arms, holding her tight to his chest. She cried against him, leaning her body into his, but she wouldn't put her arms around him. Her hands stayed clasped in her lap. "It's over, sweetie. It's over." He smoothed his hand down her back as she sobbed until she'd wrung herself dry.

He didn't know what to say or do other than hold her while she cried. Angry bile rose in his throat and frustrated helplessness zipped through him like a fly evading a flyswatter.

"It's not over. Not in my mind." Through waning tears, she looked into his eyes.

His heart clenched tightly. The sight of her puffy eyes and white-streaked cheeks crushed him. "I promise I won't let this happen again."

She unclasped her hands just long enough to squeeze his arm. "It's not your fault."

Even while she was in pain, Fortune still tried to make him feel better. He didn't though.

She quickly drifted off to sleep, so he went into the bathroom to calm down. But he couldn't. Anger eventually overtook the other emotions until all that was left was fury. His vision blurred with angry tears that turned into a screen of red, and he roared in frustration.

Seconds of silence ticked by, and he thought maybe the sound was in his own fevered mind. But then he heard Graham and Fortune's muffled voices before a knock sounded on the bathroom door. Crap, he'd woken her up.

"Jase?" Graham turned the knob until it gave way. "I'm coming in." He closed the door behind him. "What the heck is going on up here?"

"I'm gonna kill Seth."

"No, you're not."

"Yes. I am. I'm going to kill him." Jason clenched his fists, and his body followed suit, his tension ratcheting up. His thoughts were black and red blobs, and his skin was so hot he could probably start a forest fire by brushing against a tree. His full rush of emotions was just outside his active mind. The only thing keeping them at bay was his best friend's calm demeanor rippling toward him.

Graham patted him on the shoulder. "No. You're not. He was wrong, but you're not going to kill him."

Jason shook off his friend's hand. "G, I'm serious."

Graham backed away but didn't stop talking Jason down. "Jase, calm down. You can't help Fortune like this. Seth's locked up. He can't hurt her anymore. So, calm down."

"After all I've done to accommodate that jackass! And he assaults my girlfriend? What the hell!"

"Why don't we go get your car? Let's get out of here. You're disturbing Fortune, and this is as close as I ever want to be with you." Graham chuckled.

Jason relaxed his shoulders and struggled at a half-smile. He managed to get a smirk, which was reflected back to him from the giant bathroom mirror. Seeing the two of them huddled in Fortune's bathroom like gossiping teenagers would have been laugh out loud funny in any other circumstance. Now, it was just sad. Everything they'd done tonight had a veil of sadness.

They made it downstairs to the front door. Ranjan had made himself a mug of tea and was reclined on Fortune's sofa, watching something on PBS.

The urge to laugh out loud bubbled up again in Jason's gut and then died. "Ranjan, will you stay with Fortune?"

"Of course."

Graham shadowed Jason to the car as if he were a frail, old man who'd fall at any time. In reality, Jason had the strength of a teenager who'd just been wronged—virulent, incensed, and not thinking straight. Except he was thinking straight for the first time since this began. Guy assaults girlfriend. Boyfriend gets angry at guy. Boyfriend kills guy. Graham shouldn't have told him to calm down. Jason had a right to be angry.

"If Seth had done this to Dani, what would you have done?" Jason asked as they left Fortune's house.

Graham drove silently for so long, Jason wondered if Graham had even heard the question. Then he let out a heavy breath. "I would want to kill him. A few *Mortal Kombat* moves and 'Finish him!'" He barked out a laugh, then set his jaw.

"So why did you tell me to calm down?"

"Because that didn't happen to Dani."

"So, Fortune isn't as special as Dani? What the hell, G?"

"No!" Graham held up a hand. "That's not what I'm saying. I'm saying because it didn't happen to Dani, I can see things clearer than you right now, buddy. And marching off down the revenge road is not the best way to help Fortune. This is not medieval times where you duel to the death for a woman's virtue."

"Revenge road? Dueling to the death?"

Graham sighed. "Dani's got me binge-watching this show *Bridgerton* with her. Total chick bore, but she's super horny afterwards, so there's that."

"Gross. She's like a sister to me, dude."

"Well, your sister is a freak after a couple of episodes of *Bridgerton* is all I'm saying."

Jason punched Graham in the shoulder. "Dead this convo."

"I'm driving here!" Graham laughed and pulled into Beans & Bread's parking lot beside Jason's car. "Listen. This whole situation is bad. Really bad. But going after Seth is only going to make it worse. And not just worse for him. Worse for you, too. And possibly even Fortune—"

"I wouldn't do anything to hurt her—"

"I'm still talking!" Graham yelled.

Jason sighed.

"You're a forty-one-year-old man with a bad back and responsibilities—you own a small business, you want to marry somebody and start a family with them, you have parents and a sister who need you. What's going to happen if you end up in jail, huh? How's that going to work?"

Jason sat silently and let his best friend's words play in his mind. Graham was telling the truth, but Jason still wanted to bash Seth's head into the pavement. He sat for a minute in Graham's car, fuming. After a few minutes, a heavy exhale left him deflated, and a smidgen less angry. But he still wanted to punch something. "I'm going to the gym."

"Do you need me to spot you?"

"No, Mom. I don't need you to babysit me. Seth's in jail, remember? Besides, I'm going back to Fortune's after. Don't need Ranjan charming her and turning her against me."

Graham smiled, but his eyes were filled with worry. "I really am sorry this happened, Jason."

"Me too. Guess I couldn't fix this one, huh?"

He closed the door on Graham before he had a chance to respond, got in his car, and headed straight to the gym—the only way he knew how to deal right now.

He had to blow off steam somewhere, and raining blows and kicks on the gym's punching bags would be a safer alternative than denting some poor schmuck's face. When a couple of night owl fitness nuts stared at him like he was crazy, he moved to the weight benches in the far corner and kept adding weight until his arms were the consistency of rubber.

His body was tired, but his nerves still pumped anger and worry through him, and he couldn't stop thinking about Fortune's limp, fragile frame sagging in his arms. He couldn't stop the rush of guilt from overtaking him then or now. Like everything else, he'd been too late to assemble the pieces of this messed-up puzzle and figure out what was happening in enough time to right things.

Fortune had been correct about so many things lately. This time she was wrong; it was his fault. If he hadn't tried a second time to appeal to Seth's sensibilities, she wouldn't have been hurt. Jason should have cut Seth out of his life a long time ago.

The only thing he could do now was avenge her. Graham joked about dueling for a woman's virtue, but it wasn't far from what Jason envisioned.

Seth wouldn't get away with this.

Thirty-One

Fortune

WHEN SHE AWOKE IT was still night, and Ranjan was sitting in her reading chair opposite the bed. He must have drawn the babysit-Fortune straw.

"Where's Jason?" Fortune asked.

Ranjan looked away from Fortune. "Graham took him to get his car. Why don't I make you some tea? I spied your kitchen. You've got an impressive beverage station."

"Thanks. Some tea would be nice."

Ranjan turned and left the room.

Fortune called after him. "Don't think I don't know that you're lying to me, though." Jason was gone on some half-cockney mission to avenge her or some macho crap, and Graham was probably going to have to play referee. What Jason could even do was limited with Seth already behind bars. At least for the night. While it was nice to have Ranjan's ever cheerful, calming presence, it would have been nicer to have a loving and supportive boyfriend around, too. She'd probably have a lot more nights like these where sleep came in fits and spurts.

Ranjan returned with two steaming mugs. "I was telling the truth."

"Just not the whole truth?"

He touched his nose and then pointed to her.

"Jason's upset."

"Understatement." He sipped his drink. "I've actually never seen him this mad before. Talking about murder and whatnot."

Her eyes widened.

"Oh, don't worry. Graham talked him down from the ledge. And Seth is in jail, I presume?"

She nodded. Honestly, she really didn't know or care where Seth was. But she vaguely remembered a police car, and she hoped that he was shoved into the back of it and carted right off to the big house.

Ranjan settled into her reading chair, sipping his tea and sighing as if he'd just come in from a long day at the office. The word *exquisite* came to Fortune's mind as he lounged. "So, everything's going to be fine."

He wasn't telling the truth with that statement either, but Fortune chose to believe it. She drank her tea and didn't respond.

Thirty-Two

Jason

WHEN HE RETURNED TO Fortune's house, Jason walked in on a snoring Ranjan. He was fully reclined, an empty teacup perched on the sofa's console. The funny sight clanged against a wall of worry inside Jason and burst into a mental chaos.

"Oh, hey. You're back." Ranjan rubbed the sleep from his eyes and sat the chair upright. "I'd better get out of here."

"No worries. Thanks for staying with Fortune. Sorry for coming back so late. I needed to blow off some steam." Jason peered up the staircase to where it turned and disappeared to the second landing. "Is she ..." he trailed off, not knowing what he wanted to ask.

Ranjan clapped a hand on Jason's shoulder. "She'll be fine. She's strong. She'll get through this."

"Yeah." Prickling rose in his throat. "Yeah, she'll be fine."

After Ranjan left, Jason took the stairs to Fortune's room and lounged in her reading chair, dozing and tossing to get into a comfortable position. But with this ridiculous chair and his big and tall frame, there was none. He finally settled, angling away from her in a miserable approximation of a fetal position. He resembled a crumpled granddaddy spider with his arms and legs bent in awkward ways over and around the chair's arms and legs.

This was probably why, when she awoke, she giggled before she burst into a fit of tears.

"Sweetie? You okay?" Jason awoke and hovered by the side of the bed, rumpled hair and clothes, concern pressing his face into a grimace.

"No. But you don't look so hot yourself." She couldn't pull off flippant and airy any day, but especially not today. The comment came out bland and slightly accusatory.

"Well, thanks for that," he said, equally dry.

"Why were you even there, anyway? I've never seen you in that chair."

He'd never sat there before. In fact, if this were any other morning, he would be in bed with her, an arm strewn across her body or his fingers in her hair. But this wasn't any other morning; it was the worst kind of morning-after he'd ever experienced. Flashes of the night before came back unbidden, and annoyance heated his face. "I wanted to be close."

"There's closer." She tapped the rumpled mass of covers behind her where his body usually was.

He cleared his throat and looked at his feet. "I wanted to give you space."

"You just contradicted yourself." She sat up and rubbed her eyes. "This is weird. We don't even know how to be with each other anymore."

"Yeah."

He was still more than a little angry. In one night, Seth robbed the couple of more happy times together, and he had to pay for that. But as Jason looked in her sorrow-filled eyes, the pangs of guilt from the gym returned. He should've tried harder to get through to Seth instead of leaving him to stew in his own hatred. If Jason had tried harder, Seth wouldn't have unleashed his anger on her.

But he had, and it broke her. Jason couldn't fix this.

"I think I'm going to go to therapy," Fortune said into the silence.

She was going to therapy. That was wonderful. He exhaled a heavy sigh of relief, expelling some apprehension and more than a little guilt.

Fortune grabbed his hand. "I want you to go with me."

He stilled. Her hand was a rock inside his palm, and he wanted to let go of it, of the weight of what she was asking him. It was one thing to think you can fix things, it was a whole other thing to be asked to help fix something you knew you couldn't. She shouldn't have asked him to do this. He'd already proved he was out of his depth.

He took a deep breath, hoping that what he was about to say would come out right. "You probably need to do this alone. The first few appointments at least. Therapy is supposed to be a safe space, and I'm not ... that right now. I want to be that for you, but ..." He trailed off, unsure of how to form the words for the emotions zipping through his brain.

"I guess you're right about that. You've been weird ever since the hospital. We probably both need one-on-one therapy time to process all this."

The hair on the back of his neck rose, and gooseflesh dotted his sore arms so much it hurt from where he'd done way too much in the gym the night before. Working out his frustrations on punching bags was his therapy, not talking about his feelings to some stranger. And then there was the matter of Seth getting what he deserved. "I don't need therapy. I wasn't hurt. You were. I'll support you, but I'm fine."

"You're clearly not fine."

"Once I put Seth in his place, I will be." He couldn't explain it to her—he couldn't even explain it to himself—but the conviction that this was the right thing to do burned in his chest like a roasted chili pepper.

Chili peppers. He paused and thought of their first kiss when she tasted like shichimi togarashi and vanilla—hot and sweet. The only thing she'd wanted then was a gala date. He'd wanted to keep kissing her. An odd mix of emotions, a lot like the confused mix of anger and guilt and defiance he was experiencing now, clouded his thoughts. Because he hadn't talked to her about them, he almost lost her. But if he didn't fix this the right way, they weren't going to be an "us" again, and he was sure this was the right way. She needed to heal properly, and he needed to protect her while she did.

"I get that you think I'll feel better if you make Seth feel worse, but that's not how it works. He's already done damage, and I don't think I'll ever be completely over it. Protecting me or defending my honor or whatever macho thing you're thinking is not going to help that. Can you stop trying so hard to protect me and just be here?"

"This is the only way to fix things."

She slid her hand from his grasp and rose from bed, pushing him aside to face him properly. "You are still trying to be Mister Fix–it. *I'm* not a problem you solve! *We* are not a problem you solve! We are in a relationship, and we have to work through this together."

A pang of that crushing guilt resurfaced, only this time it was ten times stronger. "Fortune, sweetie, I do want to work together. I love you. We can fi—" He was about to say "fix it" when her eyes narrowed into slits.

"Jason, you know what? Just forget it. We're done." She turned away.

What was she saying? Were they breaking up? "What?"

"I said—"

"I heard what you said, and I don't accept that." He clasped her arm and shook it, so she'd face him.

Her eyes were brimming with tears. "Accept that I don't need you to fight for me now. You wouldn't pick me when I asked you to. Why on Earth would you choose me now? I mean this is not new. I'm Black, I'm fat, and now I'm damaged. Why go through therapy with someone with so many obstacles to overcome?"

"No, that's not ... I don't think of you that way. I just don't want to be in the way of your healing—"

"Just get out. You're not listening to me. I don't need this."

"Fortune, sweetie. I love—"

"Get out!" She pushed past him to the bathroom and slammed the door behind her, ending the conversation.

Afraid to make her angrier and unsure of what to do, he descended the stairs. By trying to get everyone to see they were together, he'd driven them apart. He'd broken everything he was trying to fix.

He waited for a few minutes to see if she would come down and say it was all a mistake. They would laugh for the first time in what seemed like ages, and some of the weight of all the heavy emotions they were both feeling would be lifted.

She didn't.

As he closed the door on her and her sanctuary, realization set in that he wouldn't be better without her. But he couldn't go back now.

Thirty-Three

Jason

IT WAS ALL OVER—HIS twenty-plus year friendships with his college buddies and his budding relationship with a woman he'd bought a ring for. A freaking ring, for goodness sakes. There would be no meeting each other's parents, no wedding, and no happily-ever-after with the love of his life. She was gone, and he was the reason. The weight of his sadness was painful, like someone had made him the single footer to hold up a high-rise building. In a matter of days, his life had gone from hopeful and exciting to a black hole of crushing despair. And it was all his fault.

Part of him said the practical thing to do would be to take the ring back. It was, after all, worth as much as a small car. But who cared about a car or a ring when all he wanted to do was channel Tom Hanks on some remote island talking to a volleyball because it was the only thing that couldn't get pissed at him? For the first time in his life, he was completely lost. What he'd thought would work had been a dismal failure, and what he was hoping to build in the process—a future with Fortune—had been destroyed. All because he had to be Mr. Fix-it.

He couldn't bear to face anyone outside of work or school, so he didn't bother. The result of him telling Seth to "work it out" was that the whole plan had crashed and burned.

Days passed, and Jason dragged along with them—going to work, school, and home. Rinse and repeat. He ignored texts from Graham and Ranjan asking him how he was or inviting him to The Graveyard and refused to check up on Fortune, no matter how much he wanted to.

Even though it wasn't what he'd set out to do, it felt like punishment. He was sure he'd blown up all the relationships that meant anything to him, so why would he need to talk it out? What was the purpose of coming to an understanding when he knew what they'd say? Cutting his losses would be better for all of them, especially after all of this. He had to tell them once and for all, so Graham and Ranjan would stop wasting their time texting him and inviting him out. If only he could muster up the balls to do it. For now, he would just keep ignoring and declining invites. Maybe they would get the hint and leave him be.

He was supposed to have been at The Graveyard with Graham and Ranjan. For the first time in weeks, he had even texted back promising he would be anywhere with anyone. That day he felt lighter. Celeste had been updating him on how Fortune was doing, somehow sensing that Jason needed to know even if they weren't exactly all speaking to each other. She'd made a breakthrough in therapy that day, and he couldn't have been happier. It didn't matter that they weren't exactly speaking, just knowing that she was getting better made his heart feel good. So good that he'd agreed to meet the remaining Eastcoasters for their Friday night hangout. Like old times. Sort of.

But today, as he opened his closet to pick out his favorite pair of jeans and an Arizona State t-shirt, thoughts of the last time he'd been at the bar with all of them surfaced. Jason had been struggling to understand Seth's reaction to Fortune and Fortune's argument that Seth couldn't be saved. If he had listened to her ... He couldn't will his hand to grab the jeans or his feet to walk to the t-shirt cubbies. He was paralyzed with fear—fear that his friends would demand answers from him, that he would botch cutting himself out of their lives, that the pain of ending decades-long friendships would crush him like an anvil.

After an eon of staring at his clothes and shoes, he flopped in front of the TV and began to binge-watch something. He had no idea what he was seeing, but the laugh track in the background indicated it was supposed to be funny. He wasn't laughing.

His phone pinged.

Graham: You're not here. Again.

Jason: Yeah, just not feeling it, man.

Graham: When are you going to stop hiding from us?

Jason stared at the last text from his friend for what seemed like hours. He was a raw nerve, exposed and frizzing with pain. He had been hiding, and hiding the fact that he was hiding from his friends. And obviously doing a poor job of it, because apparently, they knew. At least Graham did.

For some reason, he couldn't name, Graham's question annoyed him. The bubble of irritation grew in the pit of his stomach and rose and grew until it flared like an especially bad heartburn. He rushed off a dismissive vague text about maybe next time, prepared for the next week of work, and went to bed.

When Monday came around, the bubble of annoyance was still there, burning and stoking flickers of anger. He went about his routine, stopping at a coffee shop near his office—he couldn't step foot in Beans & Bread anymore—and doing a little administrative work before heading to today's job site—an apartment building renovation. The big commercial project they'd been working on all winter and spring had run out of money, and Jason had moved his team to another opportunity he'd won after months of bidding and re-bidding.

The annoyance bubble was now flaming into an angry fire in his chest. He could barely finish his morning rundown with the team without growling out instructions.

"Hey, boss, you good?" Austin asked after the group dispersed and started work.

"Yeah. Fine." Jason's tone was clipped and raw.

"You sure?"

"I said I'm fine, Austin." He shooed away his general contractor and turned his attention to a day laborer that was sledging into a load-bearing wall before they'd measured the temporary support wall. "Hey! Didn't I tell you not to demo this?"

"No se, señor," the day laborer responded.

"No toques esta pared! Got it? This wall," he pointed at the wall separating the kitchen and dining room. "Este es el muro que destruyes! This is the wall you should destroy!" He snatched the sledgehammer from the day laborer. "I can do it myself."

He bashed away at the partition, smashing drywall and studs. He nicked some of the plumbing, which he'd wanted to keep intact, but he didn't care. Pieces of gypsum flew as the hammer made contact with the offensive inanimate wall. "Have to do everything myself," he muttered, the wall crumbling as each blow landed. "I'm not hiding. I'm working, you jerk," he told the wall. In response, the last stud fell.

Jason dropped his arms, the sledgehammer hanging at his side. The fire in his chest was out, replaced by a dull, heavy ache. He didn't see the faces of the people surrounding him, but the stillness of the room gave away that everyone was staring at him. He looked at the debris piled around him. So much trash for one little wall, he thought.

"Get this out of here so we can put up the temporary support." He kept his eyes on the piled wood and gypsum board as he spoke. Then he turned back to the day laborer, gave him back his sledge, and left the room, searching for an unoccupied space to sort out what'd just happened.

Austin appeared from another room and approached Jason. "Hey! You want to get us thrown off this job? I don't care if you are my boss, go somewhere and simmer down before OSHA comes in here and kicks us out."

Jason stared daggers at his superintendent, but Austin didn't flinch. Without the fire stoking his actions, Jason backed down, and breathed out heavily. "I'm headed back to the office for the rest of the day."

"Good idea. Come back tomorrow with a better attitude." Austin let out a mirthless chuckle.

"Don't push it, Austin."

"Ten-four, boss."

The office was quiet when he arrived, not even Gabi or their new summer intern was around.

Austin must have called ahead and told them what happened, and they bolted.

That was fine with him; there'd be fewer people he'd be obliged to explain himself to.

He was alone. And miserable.

Doing anything to get Fortune back meant eventually going to her. But Jason wasn't ready. What would he say—what *could* he say that would even make a dent in the pain she was feeling? Pain that he'd partially caused.

He picked up his phone and dialed. "Hey, Mom," he said when his mother picked up. "I wanted to stop by for lunch tomorrow. Just to see how you and Dad are doing."

Thirty-Four

Jason

JASON LOVED HIS PARENTS, despite his strained relationship with his father when they talked about career choices. And they loved each other. So much so, he was certain part of the reason he'd never been married was because he couldn't find what his parents had. It was a friendly intimacy, an everything-is-better-when-the-other-was-around kind of vibe.

He'd never felt that way about any woman until now.

That was why he hadn't told them about Fortune. The only woman he'd ever brought home was Lily. That was when he first thought he'd made a mistake. Her in bed with his roommate Sheila confirmed his suspicions.

He pulled up the familiar driveway of the suburban ranch-er and smiled at the immaculate front yard. When it was built, this house was in the middle of nowhere, surrounded by forests on two sides and a massive farm on the third. Now it was accessed by a four-lane road with a median instead of the barely asphalted two-lane road where he used to ride his bike, was boxed in with two-storied homes on small lots, and down the street, a massive shopping center had been built, complete with Target, Trader Joe's, and several franchised casual restaurants.

But other than repairs and adding privacy fencing and hedges, his parents refused to change anything. The inside was stuck in the nineties with beige walls and warm oak wood accents everywhere—the hardwood floors, the stairs and rails to the family bedrooms. They hadn't even updated the kitchen cabinets. Jason offered more than once to get some designer friends and help them update at least the main areas, but his dad was against it.

"If we wanted to change things, I would change them," he'd said.

"But, Dad, I'm just helping out. You can lead the whole project."

"You know I can't lead a project with all this arthritis in my hands and my bad back."

Jason wanted to yell, "Thanks for the bad back genes, by the way," but he knew that would just give his dad an excuse to harp on his career choices again. So, he ended the discussion with a heavy sigh and a nod.

He rang the doorbell and unlocked the door, calling out when he entered his parents' house. Oregano, garlic, and basil aromas instantly wafted over him.

His mother yelled back from the kitchen. When he rounded the corner, he found his mother stirring a saucepan, his father sitting in the family room in his favorite chair, and his sister Skyler sitting at the island scrolling through pictures on her phone.

At times like these, he thought about just how normal his life had been before Fortune and how his normal was changing. Even though he was totally okay with that change, it had been as hard as everyone said it was.

"Hey, family." Jason rounded the kitchen island and kissed his mom's cheek. Then, he leaned over her shoulder and sniffed what she was cooking. His mouth watered. "Looks like I came just in time."

"It's the sauce for the chicken parm. What brings you by?"

"Can't I just come by just because I want to see you?"

His mom gave him a loving pat on the cheek. "Of course, you can, dear. But you don't. So, what's on your mind?" His mother's light blonde hair was mixed with gray, and she moved slower, more purposefully than she used to, but she never missed an opportunity to crack a joke. And she deadpanned better than Norm McDonald from *Saturday Night Live*.

"Wow, Mom, throw me under the bus, will ya?"

His mom laughed heartily. "You know I love you." She sat down the spoon and leaned over the island into the family room. "Jim! Food's ready!"

"Willikers, Diane! I'm not deaf."

After everyone washed their hands and took their places around the island, the family filled their plates and ate.

"Where's my favorite family member, Haley?" Jason asked his sister Skyler. Skyler was five years younger but already married. She and her husband had a nine-year-old—Jason's niece, Haley.

"She's with her father," Skyler said between bites. "They went to Romare Bearden Park for some art-in-the-park thing. Hubby saw that I needed a moment, so here I am."

Jason wished he would get to that point with Fortune, but that would require them to actually talk again, especially now that they were broken up.

"I like someone," Jason spouted. "Actually, I love her, and I want you to meet her."

"Finally. And I told you. Didn't I tell you? I told you," his mom said, smiling.

"Well, it's about time." His dad didn't look up from his plate.

"Way to go, Clooney," Skyler joked.

Jason pushed Skyler's shoulder, and she spilled sauce on the countertop.

"And that is why I couldn't get my marble." Diane handed Skyler a paper towel. "Can you act like adults? I mean you are old enough."

Skyler ignored her mother and pushed Jason back. "So, who is this mystery woman?"

"Her name's Fortune, and we've been seeing each other for almost nine months, and I want to get married, but we're going through this rough patch, and I don't know how to get back—"

"Wait a minute, what?" Diane asked. "Married?"

"She's not gay, is she?" Skyler laughed.

Jason stared at his sister blankly.

"It's about time," his dad repeated.

The rest of the family stopped eating to stare at him.

After a few moments of silence, while Jim chewed, he looked up from his plate. "What?" Jim shrugged and put his fork down. "It's true. Listen, son. You need a good woman to rein you in. You and those wild friends of yours ... Are any of you married? No. You're gallivanting around Charlotte like you're twenty–something and invincible. But you're not. You need to settle down. Face reality. Or one of you is going to end up in jail."

Jason shifted in his seat, thinking about Seth behind bars and about how close Jason came to being carted off that night, too. When he listened to Fortune, everything came into focus, his need to make everything go right, his tendency to fix things, even how he viewed his friends. And when he didn't, fighting and chaos ensued. He needed to get her back.

"Well?" his dad continued.

"What?" Jason asked.

"When are we going to meet her?"

"Oh, yeah." Jason trailed off, unsure how to answer now that his dad made his wishes clear.

I've told them I want to marry someone, and I'm pretty sure she no longer wants to marry me.

It was Lily all over again. Well, not Lily, exactly. Fortune wasn't gay and closeted, after all.

He told them everything that had happened, from meeting Fortune on SwipeMatch to their separation post-assault. Aware that his parents and little sister were his audience, he avoided mentioning either of the fights with Seth out of shame that he hadn't grown out of that adolescent behavior.

When he was in high school, Jason had been suspended so many times from school for fighting that one day his mom refused to take off work to come get him, forcing him to sit in in-school suspension until the buses began boarding. His parents warned him that he'd get into real trouble if he kept it up, and Jason didn't want to disappoint them. What he really wanted was their advice on how to get Fortune back and their approval to marry her.

One of which he didn't need, and the other they wouldn't give.

"We can't tell you how to get her back, son," his mom said. "Whatever she needs to make her feel normal again, to be safe again, you have to do that for her, and hope that she takes you back."

Jim grunted and pushed back from the island. "All I can say is that woman is a good one to put up with you. She even tried to appease that toad-boy friend of yours? Do what your mom says. Stop trying to convince her of something you can't promise and listen to her instead. You failed her once. Don't fail her again, or she's gone."

Skyler laid a gentle hand on his arm. "Wow, bro, that's *Real Housewives* level drama. Like right here in our neighborhood! You've gotta get her back, just so I can live vicariously through you." She guffawed.

Jason shook off her hand. "Cut it, sis. Can't you see I'm in pain?"

"Yeah, I don't care. Just get back with her and propose already. It's been a while since I've been to a wedding. This will be a geriatric wedding, but hey, still fun. And she sounds like she would know how to throw a good wedding." Skyler got up and put her dishes in the dishwasher. "I'm going to meet the girls for mani-pedis. Toodles."

She hugged Jim, kissed Diane on the cheek, punched Jason in the arm, and left.

"That child knows how to make an exit," Diane remarked. "Why don't you do the same, Jason? Go get this Fortune, so we can meet her."

"Wow, not subtle at all, Mom."

"Not meant to be. I love you, hun." She kissed her son on the cheek and patted his shoulder. "I know you're going to do right by her because we raised you right. But, Jason, you can't fix everything. Some things need to just stay broken."

He hugged his mom and dad, his mind reeling from hearing his mother echo Fortune's words. He had no idea how to get her back, but he did know it would have to involve calling her. Maybe flowers. Maybe begging. Probably downright groveling.

Thirty-Five

Jason

"EVERYONE IN THE BACK, break it up. Class has started."

He'd tried twice already to break up a group of kids in the back of shop class as they huddled around one student with a phone. They were watching this social media rant of someone at school—he'd recognized the brightly lit hallway behind the ranter as the math wing—and evidently disagreeing on whether he should be canceled.

"What's his problem?" a lanky student with spiked hair said.

Jason could never remember the student's name.

"He needs to be canceled."

Ashley shook her head. "Not necessary, Gene. Let him have his moment."

Oh, yeah, Eugene Collins was his name.

"This whole thing's sus."

Jason interjected yet again, raising his voice, and startling some of the students in the front of the room. "I believe I told everyone to sit down and finish their projects. This is the last day Mister Taylor has allocated for this project, and you only have a few classes after this to make sure all your projects are complete. So, anyone who's not finished with this today will have ten points taken off."

"C'mon, Mister Reed." A round-faced girl whined.

"You want to make it twenty?" Jason inwardly winced at the annoyance in his tone. His mind flashed back to the day he smashed that wall on the multi-res reno job. He couldn't lose his cool like that again, especially not in front of a class of high schoolers.

"Mister Reed ain't playin' today!" A boy with cornrows wearing the school's basketball team jersey ducked behind one of the tables in the back and got to work.

"Are you okay, Mister Reed?" Round-Faced girl glanced up at him with a mixture of sadness and confusion in her expression. She reminded him of his niece Haley when she knew she'd done something wrong and was about to be put in time out.

"I'm fine. Just get to work." Jason waved his hand with a vague dismissive air and turned away from the class for a moment. Why were young people so intense? And they had the nerve to talk to him like they were friends? He sighed. These students might be the only friends he still had if he were honest.

"I think he's lonely," Sam said in a loud whisper that absolutely everyone heard. "Maybe *he's* been canceled."

"You know, this cancel culture thing is really toxic," Round-Faced Girl said as if declaring an absolute truth that no one had figured out yet. "Besides, we wouldn't cancel you, Mister Reed. You're the chill sub."

Jason attempted a smile but was sure a grimace came out. "If you must know, I'm having an issue with my friends, and all of you berating yours has me on edge."

Ashley laughed and took her place beside her friend Sam who was putting the last coat of stain on his project. "That guy isn't anyone's friend here. He's some YouTuber loser who used to go here like four years ago. Besides, you can't cancel friends. That's why they're friends. Even if you have an argument, you can end it, and go back to being friends."

The rest of the students were focused on finishing their projects, only whispering among themselves when they needed tools or reassurance. He was always amazed at how quickly kids could go from crisis mode to focused and productive, while here he was still worried and miserable about his current state of affairs.

It had been a few weeks since he'd last seen his friends, preferring to wallow in frustration and fret over the loss of friendship. Instead, he could have been mending his relationships with Graham and Ranjan, and probably gaining a lot lower blood pressure for it.

But he needed to be sure they even wanted to mend their relationship. Maybe they wanted to punish him and formally cut him off instead, and he'd just been delaying the inevitable by hiding. The only way he'd find that out was to call Graham.

That night, Graham texted again, inviting him to The Graveyard. Ugh, it was almost Friday again. He couldn't get the days straight right now to save his life.

Instead of texting Graham back, he decided to call. He'd made the decision to face them, and he might as well start now.

"What's up?" Graham answered. In the background, a bunch of people were shouting and cursing. It sounded like he was already at the bar.

"Are you at The Graveyard? It's not even Friday, yet."

"We're still going to the basketball game Friday, right? Last game of the season. So, Graveyard, tonight. Are you coming?"

"Why do you even want me there?"

"What? What are you even asking?"

"I mean after all of this. After I busted up a friend group that's lasted over two decades?"

"Really!" Graham laughed. "You're not that major. Besides, I'm the glue of this friend group, man."

Jason chuckled. Graham's ego aside, Jason's words sounded ridiculous. He hadn't blown up his whole friendship circle, despite what happened with Seth. Though Seth was obviously cut out of the friendship, that had nothing to do with Jason. If anything, he'd just shone a light on how wrong Seth was and how he'd been holding them back all these years.

"So what? You beat up Seth—he deserved it, but still, your girlfriend dumped you because, face it, you basically told her to, and that means we, your ever-faithful stand-by-your-side-and-sing-bad-karaoke friends don't exist anymore? We're still here and, though we're not sure why, we still like you."

Graham's words hit Jason so hard his stomach clenched like he'd been punched. He wasn't as alone as he'd thought. And he hadn't broken this bond they'd forged with some problematic—but not altogether bad—group outings. "Yeah. Okay."

"Just admit it, dude. You screwed up introducing Fortune to the gang thing, and it blew up in your face. Get over it because we have."

"I'm over—well, I'm not over it, but I will be."

"Fine. Just stop ditching us when we invite you out. We didn't ditch you and your half-brained group dates." Graham laughed lightly, signaling to Jason that the group dates may have been more fun than anyone had or would let on.

Graham gave Jason the current news within their group. He was arguing with Dani again. "But we're not off!" he insisted. Ranjan had a brief lapse of judgment with some guy before going back to Darren and begging forgiveness which Darren gave him.

After catching up, Jason ended the call. He sat back on the sofa, his insides flooding with calm. The world was going from gray and black to filled with multiple colors again. This was one step in the right direction—back to happiness instead of alternating between angry and sad every day.

The past few months of group dating and drama had probably taken almost as much of a toll on them as it had on him. He'd wondered if they hated him for putting them through crazy karaoke, arcade dance battles, and watching Seth make out while superheroes battled villains. From Graham's perspective, it hadn't exactly been an awesome time, but it wasn't friendship-ending, either.

Things were shaky now. The only way he could get back to a sure friendship with the guys was to explain himself and apologize. He had to explain why he'd suggested the whole group dating thing in the first place. They needed to know why he'd been Mr. Fix–it on a hundred.

Just because he couldn't fix something didn't mean it would stay broken. Maybe it hadn't even been broken in the first place. His dad still loved him even though Jason didn't choose the path his dad had wanted. Graham and Ranjan were still texting him despite everything Jason had done to push them away. His class had been right—real friends don't cancel you.

But what about real loves? In all this time, he hadn't even apologized to Fortune, the one person who had been hurt the most by this whole cluster. He'd been so weighed by guilt and not wanting to put any of it on her that he hadn't said anything. He thought supporting Fortune by giving her space and keeping his feelings to himself was enough.

But as the relief and warmth flooded through his bones again after only fifteen minutes of reconnection with Graham, Jason could practically taste the goodness of reuniting with Fortune. And the only way he'd get to experience that would be with an apology. He could use the apology session with his friends as a practice round because the one with Fortune would be ten times harder.

Let the apology tour begin.

Thirty-Six

Jason

THEY WERE GOING TO the basketball game the next day, so he invited Graham and Ranjan to his place under the guise of having a drink before the game and offering to drive. Offering to chauffeur in Charlotte's after-game traffic was sure to get at least Graham over. Graham and Ranjan agreed to bring Dani and Darren, though Jason stressed that it wouldn't be a group date.

"I'm never doing those again," Jason declared. Why he'd thought the group dates would fix anything was a puzzle he'd leave unsolved.

"I actually kind of liked them. The ones at the beginning, anyway," Graham said.

When the foursome arrived, Jason had wound himself into a frenzied knot and eaten a third of another cheesecake Fortune had left. Ranjan and Darren came in first, laughing at some joke they must have shared on the way in. *They look so in love.* A pang of missing Fortune pounded him square in the gut, and he wished this nightmare of being without her would be over soon.

Dani and Graham came in shortly after, arguing about something Graham deemed "so trivial, I don't know why we're even talking about it."

Dani ignored him and said hello to Jason.

"Hi, Dani," Jason responded. "You okay?"

She shot a venomous stare at Graham. "See? That's how a caring boyfriend is supposed to act! Ask me how I'm feeling once in a while."

"Oy vey," Graham sighed.

"You're not Jewish."

"Here ya go, buddy." Jason shoved a beer into Graham's hand. "Have a cold one."

Graham accepted the beer and sat at the kitchen island beside a standing Jason.

Dani had already claimed an armchair by the door.

Jason shielded a chuckle from his friends.

Time to man up, Reed. He cleared his throat. "Listen, guys..." he cleared his throat again, aware of his faux pas. "And Dani. I kind of lied about tonight."

"There's no basketball game?" Darren asked.

Was that a hint of hopeful Jason detected in Darren's tone? Jason hid a grin. "Yeah, there's a basketball game. I lied about the reason I asked you over."

Graham held his beer aloft. "Where's the lie? You are still driving, right?"

"I meant that's not the only reason I wanted you to come." He took another swig of his beer, hoping it would boost his courage or at the very least jog some apologetic phrases loose. He hated apologizing, but he hated being without his friends even more. "I needed to explain about the group dates. And why I don't want to do them anymore. They were me trying to fix something I shouldn't have been messing with in the first place. So, I'm sorry for putting you guys through that."

He paused, looking around the room at his smaller but truer friend group. They were intently listening with expressions of openness and acceptance. Warmth flooded his insides. He could do this, possibly without bloodshed, so he plowed further.

"I'm so used to getting people to believe in my vision or fixing it when they can't see it that I didn't realize I couldn't fix people's beliefs. I couldn't believe that you, Dani, and Tina thought Fortune was aggressive." He nodded Dani's way. "And I didn't understand why Seth couldn't grow to love Fortune, especially after all of you eventually did. I mean, you all came around, right?"

No one offered a word of response.

Jason continued, "Yeah. Got it. You didn't come around. You each formed your own feelings about her ... about us, despite us being some 'ensemble show on ABC.'" He threw a knowing smirk in Ranjan's direction. "And I'm okay with that."

He really was okay. For the first time since the awkward friends' dinner, he'd accepted that everyone wouldn't fall in love with Fortune. What mattered was that he had. "It doesn't matter how much you like Fortune," he said with a conviction he actually felt. "What matters is that I love her. And I'm glad I have people in my life who respect that."

Silence fell over the room. Everyone looked at each other and then at Jason, as if daring another to speak first.

Well, Reed, you really know how to kill a good mood.

Ranjan broke the silence. "Well, I love the woman. But you know that already." He made his way to Jason. "I am glad you realize that you don't need our approval, though. Because I'm going to date whoever I want, and to heck with y'all, as they say."

Darren piped up. "Ahem?"

"And the person I want to date is Darren." He peered at Darren out of the corner of his eye.

"Thank you!" Darren punctuated.

Ranjan shook his head. "So needy, that one."

Everyone laughed, and the tension in the room dissipated.

"The point is, we're your friends, regardless. If you say she's the one for you, we believe you." Ranjan threw an arm around Jason, and they hugged for the first time in years. "Now, where is she?"

That was a whole other conversation Jason had to have.

By the time the group made it to their seats the game was halfway through the first quarter. Charlotte was up by twelve points, but it was way too early to make any predictions. It was kind of like the state of Jason's new friendship dynamic.

For the first time since college, there was no Seth, and everyone had a significant other.

Yeah, right. He didn't actually have Fortune anymore.

Graham eased into the seat next to Jason, holding a beer that was half froth and about to spill over the cup's edge and cradling a clear plastic container of loaded nachos. The acrid wheaty aroma of the beer clashed with the heavy meaty smell of the nachos, and Jason had to mentally tamp down the urge to knock the food out of Graham's hand.

"You never said where Fortune was," Graham said before sipping the froth off his beer. "This could have been Group Dates two point oh."

Jason chuckled. "Even if it had been, I would never call it that. Group dates is like a curse word around here." He cleared his throat. "She's ... I haven't spoken to her since she started therapy."

Graham stopped mid-bite and put down his loaded nacho. "What? Then what was all this explaining and apologizing for?"

"We're ..." He huffed. "We're giving each other some space. At least that's what I think we're doing. It's just temporary." He hoped so, at least.

"What did you do? Because she was talking to you after the incident. She didn't need space then."

So, this is what they were calling Seth's assault now. The incident. As if it were some small mistake instead of the life-changing disaster he was sure it was. The tiny hairs on his arms rose with even the indirect mention of what happened that night. "I didn't do anything!"

"Maybe that's the problem—she asked you to do something, and you didn't. What's the one thing she asked you to do that you haven't done?"

Jason thought back to their last conversation. It had dissolved when he'd balked at therapy. He hadn't wanted to get in the way of her healing, but really, he didn't see any need to go. He'd wanted revenge against Seth instead. "She asked me to go to therapy with her."

"Then that's what you have to do. Go to therapy with her. Apologize there."

Charlotte scored, and the crowd got on its feet, but Jason stayed seated. Graham's explanation was simple. Too simple. But, since Jason had no other ideas, he'd take simple any day.

Two-thirds of the way through the game, Ranjan and Darren left, Ranjan said because Darren had a headache. Jason smiled, knowing that Darren really didn't like basketball.

After the game was over, Jason honored his promise by driving Dani and Graham home in their car, then taking a Lyft back to his place where the group had originally met.

The whole way home, Jason thought about apologies. He was never good at them, and in this case, he was sure an apology would make things worse. Fortune would relive the assault just as she was getting over it with therapy. He played through scenarios of how long he could go without meeting her at therapy to apologize and what would happen if he didn't, but he kept coming back to Graham's words. There was no way around it; Jason had to apologize to get her back. And the only way he could do that would be to go to therapy.

It was late, but he had to do it now before he got home and talked himself out of it. He dialed Celeste, and she picked up on the first ring. "Jason? What's going on? It's almost midnight."

"I'm sorry to call so late, but I need to do this before I lose my nerve. Can you deliver a message for me?"

"Okay." Celeste said the word as if it had four syllables instead of two.

"Please ask Fortune if she still wants to do joint therapy because I'm ready."

Thirty-Seven

Jason

A FEW DAYS AFTER Jason's midnight plea, Celeste arranged a meeting between him and Fortune at Celeste's house. His parents lived close to Celeste and Mauricio, but it was a world away in prestige and style. The Parisis weren't playing around with their gated community entrance, full brick façade, and semicircular driveway.

When he saw Fortune's car, his heart sped up, and he forgot his awe over the million-dollar estate. Thoughts of seeing her again overtook his mind—her vanilla scent, her luscious curves, her sexy alto saying risqué things and murmuring in pleasure. It had been weeks since he'd even been near her, and his hands itched, wanting to touch her. *Calm down, Reed. You're not forgiven yet.*

He approached the door and rang the bell. Celeste answered, all smiles and elegance. She was wearing some flowy, multicolored thing—not a dress but not *not* a dress—which gave her an air of sophistication. "Welcome to our home!"

Jason felt underdressed in his usual cargo pants, a t-shirt, and work boots. At least his boots were clean. Still, he followed suit and left them by the door with the rest of the shoes there. "Thank you for having me." He gave her a friendly hug.

"Come on back to the kitchen. Fortune just got here."

He followed her through the modern-style foyer, which was bigger than in most houses this size, but when he saw the custom offices on both sides, it made sense. In fact, everything made sense here, from architecture to design choice. It gave you a comfortable, relaxing feeling as if you were at your own home. But he spotted the custom furnishings and the high-end finishes that conveyed to him that he was not in fact at home and not to touch anything he couldn't afford to replace. "You have a lovely home," he said with as much coziness as he could muster.

"Thanks! We like it."

He'd hope so. "When did you ..." He stopped short. Fortune was perched on a stool in front of him, nibbling on a piece of cheese from one of two huge charcuterie boards piled high with snacks.

"Fortune," he breathed at the sight of her, struggling to slow his racing heart. He stopped wondering why he reacted like this. He was in love with her, and this is what being in love felt like.

She turned and met his gaze. "Jason. Hey."

"Hey."

They stared at each other for a minute or ten.

God, she looked good, he thought, stilling his hands by his sides. He missed her so much it hurt being this close and not being able to touch her.

Celeste cleared her throat, and the spell was broken. "Jason, have a seat." She sat a plate in front of the seat beside Fortune.

He edged in by her and reached in to fill his plate. His side brushed the outside of her thigh, and lightning went through him from that point. He looked over at her. "How've you been?"

"Good," Fortune looked at her plate, and he wanted to tilt up her chin so she had to stare at him. "Not good. I mean better. Better than since you last saw me."

"I'm glad you're improving." He focused on Celeste so he wouldn't get lost in dreaming about Fortune. "Celeste, are we expecting more guests? This is a real spread you've got here."

"Only moi." Celeste's husband, Mauricio, entered from the foyer. "And only for a minute. Tesoro mio loves making charcuterie boards every chance she can get." He kissed his wife softly on the cheek, and her face brightened.

A pang of jealousy hit Jason, and he smiled to hide it. He glanced at Fortune again who was looking lovingly at her best friend. Did she wish to have that feeling with him? Or had she given up on them being together?

Mauricio turned to Jason. "It is good to see you both again." He smiled. "We'll hopefully see more of you in the future, yes?" He raised an eyebrow at Jason.

"I hope so," Jason answered as he gazed at Fortune.

She looked back at her plate.

"Well, I'm going to take this handsome man upstairs and convince him that it's his turn to do laundry. Cheeto! Sunshine!" The Parisis exited the kitchen and went up the stairs, fur babies following in their wake.

"Fortune, I ..."

She threw up her hand. "Before you start, I have something to say."

Jason sat and ate, yielding the floor to her.

"I know you've been checking up on me, and I'm not sure how I feel about that. But Celeste convinced me you had good intentions. She also convinced me this was orchestrated with those same good intentions."

"I promise. All good here."

"I need assurance that you're not going to talk about revenge or killing anyone. I can't have you in that headspace if we're going to do therapy."

He nodded. He replayed those two days in his mind, appalled at his behavior. It was ridiculous to him now. He'd acted like a Neanderthal, but to her it was probably counterproductive and even a little scary. "I promise I won't go there. I'm not in that headspace anymore."

"Good. Okay. Good." She rubbed her palms on her jean-clad thighs. She was nervous around him, and that made him sad.

He took one of her hands in both of his, and she matched his stare. "Fortune, I miss you. I need you in my life. And if that means therapy to be with you again, I'll do it. Whatever you want, I'll do it because I love you."

"I'm glad you want to do this, but you have to want it for you too, not just for me. You were really angry that night."

"I know. I promise you. I'm not that angry anymore. I'm done. I'd never hurt you. You know that, right?"

She nodded.

"Can I kiss you?"

"Yes." She closed her eyes and leaned towards him. Instead of kissing her on the mouth, he touched his lips to her cheek. In that moment, with her intoxicating scent swirling around him and her soft cheek like a welcome caress, a flood of their times together rushed into his thoughts. The heat of her cheek warmed the deepest parts of him, even the parts he thought would be cold and closed off forever. He had to do whatever it took to get her back. Nothing felt better than this. He couldn't survive without it again.

A mousy, slim woman with long sandy blonde hair pulled back in a ponytail, Dr. Chastain was dressed like a middle-school guidance counselor in tan chinos and a peach button-down blouse. She was a hugger, which usually wasn't a big deal for Jason. He was a hugger, too. But something about Dr. Chastain embracing him seemed weird. Like she was being overly accepting of him when she barely knew him, and when even his own girlfriend—ex-girlfriend?—wouldn't even hold his hand. Fortune sat on the far end of one of the two sofas in the room literally holding herself in—her legs were crossed at the ankle and her arms were crossed over her chest. It reminded him of the morning after their first night together. She had closed herself off then too, not even entertaining the notion that he'd want her for more than just a one-night stand. He thought he'd made headway last week at Celeste's. Evidently, not. This was not the way to start a reconciliation.

"Hello, Jason, glad you could join us." Dr. Chastain smiled and motioned towards the sofa where Fortune sat.

"Nice to meet you, Dr. Chastain," he answered, taking a seat on the opposite end of the sofa.

"So, Jason, tell us why you're here." She picked up a pad and a pen from the desk behind her and sat in the chair in front of the desk, facing him.

"I want to apologize to Fortune."

"Why?" She leaned in slightly and focused on him.

"Because she's hurt because of me."

"Fortune told me that a guy named Seth assaulted her, and that's why she came to see me."

"Seth was my friend. By insisting everyone get along, I created the situation. She got assaulted because I was caught up in trying to convince everyone that we could be friends, but I made everything worse." He shook his head and turned to Fortune. "I'm sorry. I didn't see it."

Fortune turned her head to meet his gaze, but her body was still closed off, burrowed in the couch's corner. "I told you about him. And you didn't listen to me." Her words smarted like the sting of running into a holly bush. "Why didn't you listen to me?"

"I didn't really get it that he was a racist. I just thought—I mean, how did we not see this? He's always been a jerk, but I didn't ... he had never attacked ... I just thought he was upset about some of his work stuff and was projecting it. I didn't realize Seth was rotten. That he couldn't be fixed. That I can't fix everyone. They are who they are. And only they can change themselves," Jason declared.

She exhaled a heavy breath. "It's not—it shouldn't have been about him. It should have been about me. It should have been about us." Fortune ground out those last words as if she had to drag them through her body to express them.

Was it that hard for her to ask to be a priority? The point was she shouldn't have had to ask; she was his girlfriend.

"Do you know how hard it is being a Black woman?" She shook her head. "No, you don't. It's hard. We're not respected for our ideas. We're not valued for our contributions to society. We're not even seen as desirable on dating apps." She flashed a wry smile and shook her head. "Sometimes you need someone in your corner to believe you when you say you need help instead of trying to help someone else."

"But I did believe you. I was meeting Seth to tell him so."

"No, you didn't believe me! I told you that you couldn't fix Seth, and that you were going to have to choose, but what did you do? You tried to fix Seth. My own boyfriend didn't want to see my side of the picture."

Was that what he had done?

She continued, "When I told you we need to stop doing the group dates, you said, 'No, I'm going to figure out what Seth's problem is.' When he said he's going to stop doing them, you fight with me about it? How is that believing me? How do you think I felt?"

"I'm sorry I didn't see this. I'm sorry I let him hurt you. I didn't know what to do. I thought I was doing the right thing. I ..."

"So, it was about him, not me."

"Sweetie, no. That wasn't it at all. I ..."

"Why didn't you pick me? You said you would pick me!" She wrapped her arms around her stomach and rocked back and forth, her voice barely above a whisper.

He was stunned. Instead of accepting or rejecting his apology, she'd somehow thought something even worse. That he hadn't even cared about her in all of this.

"But I did choose you. I ended my friendship with him." He reached out to her, but she didn't reach back, instead holding herself tighter. "I asked Seth to meet me at Beans & Bread that night to tell him I had picked you and wanted to marry you. He told me not to. We ended our friendship then. I didn't know he was that angry or that he would take it out on you." Now she knew the truth. He hadn't met with Seth to fix things. He went for a round of bare-knuckled truth-telling and a side of demanding acceptance.

"You should have fought for me. From the beginning." Fortune sniffed. Her eyes glistened, and her lips bunched and twisted until they resembled the end of a corkscrew. A tear escaped and slid down her cheek. "Why didn't you fight for me? For us?"

If he had treated her like she was a priority instead of part of a puzzle to solve, then he would have listened to her and dealt with Seth before any of this happened. Jason's stomach churned so violently at her tears and anguished whispered words that his abs cramped.

As he sat on the opposite end of the couch from Fortune, closer than he'd been in months outside of Celeste's place, he realized he was still too far away. This wasn't the start of a reconciliation; it was the beginning of the end. His heart hurt so much, he was sure it was breaking in two. "Fortune, I love you. I—"

Dr. Chastain cut in. "Jason, Fortune, I know this is painful for both of you, but believe me, this is progress." She glanced at her watch. "Our time is up for today."

Thirty-Eight

Jason

DESPITE GOING TO SEVERAL more sessions with Fortune and Dr. Chastain, Jason was no closer to getting Fortune back. His apology clearly hadn't cut it for her, and he had no idea what would.

He was taking everyone's advice, but somehow it hadn't worked. Not that he was trying to fix things again, but ... he couldn't help that. It was who he was.

It was who *he was*.

Something about that kept ringing in his head until it clicked: who he was had gotten in the way of who he wanted to be with Fortune. And he needed help to get out of his own way.

Jason thought back to the night that changed them forever. The ER doctor had said, "Anger is coming off you in waves. You'll need your own therapist." He had ignored him then, but now he regretted not taking the doctor's advice.

Calling Dr. Chastain to ask for a referral was the last thing he wanted to do—no, going to therapy was the last thing he wanted to do—but he swallowed the lump in his throat and did it. She'd given him the name of a Dr. Farragut like it was nothing and wished him well. He was a child being ushered to a new classroom.

"So, it says here that your girlfriend's had some trauma, and you're helping her through it." Dr. Farragut scrolled through Jason's online intake form on a computer tablet with the rubber ball top of a pen. He looked over his clear plastic-rimmed glasses at Jason and waited for confirmation.

"Yes. I got your name from Doctor Chastain who we've been seeing for joint therapy."

"So, what's that been like for you?"

Jason didn't answer for a few moments, wondering if he should tell the truth or sugarcoat it. Lying would only get him a $200 bill and no progress to show for it. He was here for help. "It's been hard. At times I'm not even sure why I'm there. I don't want to be crass, but I want to say, 'I'm not the one who got assaulted. She was. I don't need to be here.'"

"So, why are you here?"

"Because I want her back."

"You're not together?" Dr. Farragut switched his tablet for a pad, flipped his pen, and began writing.

"No." Jason peered at his shoes to avoid Dr. Farragut's scrutiny. "We broke up because I wanted to kill the guy, but she wanted me to go with her to therapy."

"So why not stay broken up? I mean, there are other fish in the sea, right? Why endure this thing you don't want to do just to get her back?"

Jason's head snapped up. "Are you seriously asking me?"

"That's what you pay me for." The corners of his mouth tipped up.

"Because she's the one. She's the one I'm meant to be with."

"Don't you think she could be thinking the same thing? That you're the one she wants to be with, so she wants you to be okay, too? I take it you don't go around wanting to kill people all the time."

"No."

"And you didn't want her to be assaulted."

"Of course not."

"So maybe, you were affected by this, too. Of course, you weren't as traumatized as she was, but your aberrant reaction signals that you didn't come out of this unscathed. You said you were angry. Did you also feel guilty? Maybe because you couldn't stop or prevent what happened?"

Guilt. He was plagued by it still, unable to shake it away every time he sat on Dr. Chastain's couch. "Yeah. I've got guilt." Then he spilled the story about Seth and the group dates and how it was his idea and how, for a while, he'd blamed himself for what happened, but he only recently let go of that notion.

"Why did you blame yourself?"

"Because I had to go be Mister Fix-it. If I hadn't tried to fix Seth and Fortune's friendship, he wouldn't have gotten angrier with her."

Dr. Farragut took a moment to let that reasoning float in the ether. Then he trained his stare on Jason. "Tell me about why you feel you have to fix things."

At first, Jason couldn't articulate a reason. Blurry images of past times where he was called on to fix something flew around his mind, but nothing stuck. And then his father's face came into clear view.

Compelled by some strange niggling in the depths of his thoughts, he told Dr. Farragut about his father's disapproval of his career choice. As much as he wanted to dam them up behind that invisible wall in his brain, the words flowed.

"I believed the trades were the family legacy. Dad and Granddad said as much in the amount of pride they had for their work. They were always the ones neighbors would come to for help with their house projects, especially the ones that went wrong.

"So, when I found that I loved woodworking, I knew Dad would be proud of me wanting to go into the family business." He sniffed and looked at his hands in his lap, suddenly unable to look Dr. Farragut in the eye. "I thought ... he would hesitate for a minute after I told him, then crack that half smile he does when he's proud of something and suggest schools or even ask me to be his apprentice."

Choked laughter came out like a cry from his throat. "But that wasn't what happened. He did not approve. He said, 'Watching your grandfather struggle with his job and crippling arthritis, and then me having to take an early retirement when the housing bubble burst, it was tough. Luckily, I had my MBA to fall back on. Unlike my dad, I had a plan for the downtimes.'"

They'd been at the dinner table, discussing work and school and futures. Jason held an acceptance packet from Arizona State University in his hands, and he had been extolling the virtues of their Construction Science major to the family. He thought his father would complain about him choosing a school across the country from their Charlotte home. Instead, he harped about Jason's proposed major. "But Dad, I love working with wood. And even if there are slumps, I can make it."

"You need to get an office job. Become a manager of something." His father went back to his dinner.

"Dad, you're not listening."

"I'm not going to pay for you to go clear across the country to mess up your future! Choose another major or think about another school."

Jason and his dad compromised. His dad agreed to pay for an ASU education if Jason minored in something else. He chose Business Administration to show that he had been listening, but he was determined to show his dad that a career in construction was going to work for him. Jason graduated with honors. When he set up his own company back at home in Charlotte in a tiny one-room office in a multi-tenant building, he even had a party to celebrate his accomplishments.

"But Dad didn't attend any of it. He didn't even acknowledge what I'd done! Every time I brought up the job with him, he'd criticize me or talk down to me. When I told him I'd gotten my first commercial project, Dad said, 'You're not going to make it to retirement age if you keep at this.'"

He wiped his nose with the back of his hand. "I knew then that he didn't really get how much I loved my career. He was seeing it through his eyes and not mine."

Silent tears ran down Jason's cheeks as he sat and absorbed the memory he'd just shared. Until now, he hadn't told anyone what happened. He hadn't even fully examined it himself. But there it was. Ironically, Jim Reed had made Jason Mr. Fix-it by opposing his career choice.

Dr. Farragut handed Jason a box of tissues from a side table. "Sometimes a person can be altered so much by someone or something that everything they see is like seeing through a permanent filter. No matter how different the current situation may be—every comment, gesture, interaction is viewed through that person's filter. Like Seth. Like your father. Like you."

He took off his glasses. "Jason, you trying to fix things was not about addressing Seth's hurt. It was about your own. Only when you address this issue with your father, can you begin to see things in a different way. Fortune wants to be with the real you. Not Mister Fix-it."

Thirty-Nine

Jason

JASON LEFT DR. FARRAGUT'S office with a clarity he'd never experienced before. Who knew reconciling with Fortune meant having to reconcile with Jim Reed? What Jason thought should've been about Fortune and Seth and racism was about him and his dad. He'd become Mr. Fix–it all because his dad didn't want him to be. And being Mr. Fix-it for relationships he couldn't and shouldn't have been fixing was what got him in this mess to begin with. He was alone because he was trying to prove something to a man who couldn't care less.

He wrestled with this new self-discovery for weeks, unable to get up the nerve to talk to his dad.

Then one day after another intense session with Dr. Farragut, he realized he was ready. When he got into his car, he called his parents' house.

"Hello?" his mother answered.

"Hey, Mom. Is Dad there?"

He heard shuffling on her end and a door slam. "Yes, he's here. Jim? Your son wants to talk to you." His mother's tone went from cheerful to flat. Clearly, she wasn't wasting her happy voice on one of her kids.

Jason smiled at his phone.

"How ya doing, son?" His dad sounded like he was readying for a battle. Of course, most of their discussions lately had been small battles. He thought again about his dad's advice on getting Fortune back. Even that had sounded accusatory and antagonistic at the same time he was trying to be helpful.

He wasn't going to give in to battling his dad today. He needed to forgive him.

"I'm okay, Dad. I need to talk to you, though."

"Well, come on by the house. I'm just tinkering on the old rust bucket outside."

"Thanks, Dad."

When Jason arrived, his dad was where he'd said he would be, in the garage under the hood of a classic '68 Ford Mustang that looked neither rusty nor old. Jim Reed had been quietly pouring his heart into keeping his "little Milly" up and running since he'd bought it when he was sixteen. If home values hadn't skyrocketed in the past decade, little Milly would be worth more than their house. Jason looked around the garage, which was missing sheetrock in places and had oil stains on the concrete.

"What brings you by?" his dad asked. The sound of the ratchet wrench and socket he was using to take out a spark plug almost drowned him out.

"I need to talk to you about Arizona State."

"What about it? Are you going back there? Do you need money?"

"No." This probably wasn't the best place to start this conversation, but it was the only way he knew. "Do you know why I went out there?"

"You wanted to get away from me."

Jason breathed deeply and shook his head even though his dad couldn't see him. "No, Dad, I didn't." He leaned back against the workbench where his dad had retired his carpentry tools along with his business license. He hadn't even asked Jason if he'd wanted to take over the business when he retired. At the thought, a burning wound through Jason's gut into his chest. "I wasn't trying to get away from you. I was trying to find me."

"Were you out there?"

"What?"

"In Arizona. Were you out there? Did you find yourself out there?"

"No. I mean, yes! I didn't find myself exactly. I found freedom. To be me."

"What's this about, son?" Jim straightened from under the car's hood and looked at Jason squarely. His dad's hair was a salt and pepper gray, and the lines on his forehead as he scowled reminded Jason of claw marks. The man leaned slightly to the left, favoring his left leg, and was pitched forward in a stoop, as if he was having trouble straightening his back. They were like battle scars from war, but for Jim Reed, the war was the thirty years he'd spent in construction.

Jason wondered if this is what he'd be like in another twenty-five years.

"Are you coming out or whatever they call it? Are you telling me Fortune's a man?"

Jason guffawed. "No! Fortune's definitely a woman. I'm not coming out, but I need to tell you something I think I've been trying to tell you for years. Ever since I came back from Arizona State." He cleared his throat, withering a little under his dad's scrutiny. "Dad, I wanted to tell you I'm sorry if I disappointed you. I know you didn't want me to go into construction, but I loved carpentry. I had to see if I could make a living at it because why not do something I've always wanted?"

Jim Reed put down the wrench and let down the car's hood. "Go on, then."

Jason stood tall again, moving away from the workbench. "So, I opened the company and did just that. I make a good living, and I'm happy doing what I do. But I think ... I think I've always wanted you to acknowledge that. Because if you had, it would be a sign that things were fixed between us."

"Son ... Jason, things were never broken between us. I was warning you not to throw your life away. A career in construction is a hard road. You didn't have to make a living that way, but you did, anyway. I wasn't disappointed in you; I was worried for you. I still am. I'm always worried something's going to happen to you on a construction site and you end up killed or hurt. Or you're just going to get to the point where you've messed yourself up so much—" he rubbed his lower back, "that you're going to spend your retirement in pain. And what was it all for? A few dollars in the bank and a gold watch?"

"But we're not the same, Dad. Except maybe our backs." He chuckled wryly. "Construction isn't just about a few dollars to me. It's about spending time doing something I love. And they don't give out gold watches anymore, so I've got to love it even more."

He laughed, and his father smiled a little, too. Maybe Jason was getting through to him.

"All this time I've been trying to fix things. Anytime someone had a problem, I was always there ready with a solution. But this time instead of fixing things with my girlfriend, I broke them completely. I've been wondering why I couldn't fix things with her until now." He took a step toward his dad. "I've got to let go of trying to fix us. I've got to forgive you to get her back."

Jim raised an eyebrow. "Forgive me? All I've done is look out for you!"

Jason held up both hands. "Dad! Dad. I'm not saying you have to apologize. I'm saying ..." He let out a heavy breath. "I'm saying I have to be okay with you not liking my career choices. You have your reasons, and I need to stop trying to get you to see my side. I need to stop trying to fix us. This thing about my job is always going to be between us, and I need to be okay with that."

A pang of sadness beat through Jason as a defeated, re-signed expression clung to his father's features. Even though he couldn't fix them, he certainly didn't want to hurt his dad's feelings. But he wanted Fortune back. Life wasn't life without her.

"I want her," Jason said. "That means I have to forgive you and be okay with you. And I am."

"I understand. You know, walking in your grandpa's foot-steps was hard for me. According to him, I could never live up to the standard of excellence he set with his construction business. Believe it or not, I wanted to be a writer."

"What? I didn't know that."

"Yep. Your grandpa told me he wouldn't pay for me to throw my future away on some dream, and if I didn't go to trade school so I could take over the business one day, I'd have to find a way to go to college on my own. Who would defy the great James Reed, Senior? Not me. Not anyone. I grew to like construction, but I never loved it. I couldn't see how anyone could love it. And then, with the early onset of arthritis in my leg and the slipped disk in my back, I was done at fifty-nine."

Jim grabbed his son by the shoulders. "I'm sorry, Jason. I thought I was doing the right thing by keeping you from that life. I didn't understand how much you loved carpentry. I was letting my own feelings and experience cloud my judgment. I'm sorry for my response to your decision, but don't ask me to be sorry for worrying about you. I'm never going to stop that."

"I know, Dad. And I forgive you."

Jim pulled his son into a hug so tight Jason could barely move. He hadn't felt this loved in a long time. Comforting warmth emanated from his dad and blanketed Jason, and he wanted to stay rooted to the spot for as long as he could. "We should have done this sooner."

"Yes, Dad. We should have."

Forty

Jason

AFTER HIS FIRST THERAPY session alone, Jason found his joint sessions with Fortune easier and less stressful. He and Fortune became more comfortable around each other. So much so that they started seeing each other outside of Dr. Chastain's office. He wouldn't call it dating—he didn't want to dredge that up again—but he did enjoy whatever it was they were doing.

They'd revisited all the places she loved—parks, museums, Blackhawk Hardware—but every time they returned home, they parted. She'd reach towards him, but as soon as she got close, she'd step back, as if she were calculating how much courage she'd need to show some physical intimacy. And every time she backed away, he second-guessed what they were doing, worried he was triggering her and derailing her progress in therapy. In the end, he'd settle for a friendly hug when she'd give him that now-familiar, confused look, trying not to let on that he was confused, too.

That afternoon, they'd been at a stone yard on the hunt for a new countertop for Fortune's kitchen. She said she'd needed an expert, but really, she wanted his validation. He smiled inside at the thought.

They were at her front door again, as awkward as two high school teenagers on their first date. She reached out to him. "Thanks for hanging out with me today."

He stepped close and enveloped her in a hug. "Sure thing. I'll see you tomorrow, okay? We're meeting Ranjan and Darren for drinks at Blue. That is if you want." After a moment, he moved towards his car, but she still held tight.

"Sweetie, you okay?" He leaned back to peer into her eyes.

"Don't go," she whispered.

"Did something happen?"

"No. I—"

He framed her face with his hands. "He's locked up. He can't hurt you again. You know that, right?"

"Just stay, okay?"

"Okay, I'll stay." Did staying mean what he thought it meant? He brushed his palm over her cheek and lowered his head to kiss her.

Though the first brush of their lips was softer than feathers, lightning coursed through him at their touch. It had been months since they'd really kissed, and his body awoke at the memory of her. Too awake for a chaste peck on the lips. He pulled her into him at her waist, curling her against him but shifting his lower half away. Calm down, Reed, he mentally chastised himself. But she was Fortune. He couldn't imagine ever not getting turned on by her taking charge and asking for what she wanted. Still, he didn't want to scare her away, especially after they'd made so much progress. The threads of their relationship were still reforming, and everything was fragile, easily broken. He didn't want to snap them again.

Her hands shaking as she wrapped her arms around him gave him the first clue that she didn't want this. She may have wanted him, but sex was off the table. Then her whole body shivered in his embrace and not a good shiver. She was spiraling. He'd read this wrong, and if he didn't back away now, he'd probably derail her therapy.

He released her and made a move to leave. "Sweetie, we don't have to do this. I'm fine. I'll see you at therapy next week. I don't want to pressure you. I promise I'm fine if we say goodnight now."

When her forehead creased ever so slightly, he stopped short.

"But I'm not," she said in a whisper.

He lingered, hoping for ... what, exactly? For her to magically get over her fear and confusion? For another taste of her lips? His eyes locked in on those lips, now pursed in a full, tight line.

"I don't want you to go," she said.

Something clicked in his mind at her statement—his mother's words came back to him, "Whatever she needs to make her feel normal again, to be safe again, you have to do." It wasn't about him, or her being comfortable with him. It was about what she wanted. He thought that he should leave and give her some space. But now he knew that was wrong, too. Like his dad had told him to, he was listening to Fortune now—everything she said in her words, her expressions, and her actions told him she didn't need him to fix the situation or give her space. He needed to do whatever she needed to feel normal again. He needed to just stay with her.

He grasped her shoulders and bent to face her and hold her gaze. "Fortune, I'm listening. I get it now. I can't fix this, but I'm not abandoning you because I can't. I get that it's going to take time for you to be comfortable with me again, and I'll be right here waiting when you do. I love you, and I hear you. I promise. I really do hear you this time."

Fortune blinked, as if blinking helped her register what he was saying. The crease between her brows smoothed, and her pursed lips widened into a smile that warmed his heart and slowed his pulse from an anxiety-ridden level back to normal. She kissed him softly on the corner of his mouth and then leaned back.

"Thank you." She breathed, her relief palpable.

"How about we binge a few episodes of *Golden Girls*?"

"Great idea. I'll get the Moscato; you get the cheesecake."

He released her shoulders but didn't move. Instead, he watched her retreating back as she went to the kitchen. For the first time in months, he felt relaxed. Normal, even. Like he'd gotten his dream job, and he no longer had to impress anyone. He only had to be himself and allow everyone else to be who they were.

"I told you to stop staring at my ass!" she yelled from behind the open refrigerator door.

He shook his head and chuckled under his breath. "Never going to happen, sweetie," he said as he joined her.

Dr. Chastain's outfit almost matched her office drapes today—a pastel pink and yellow frilly blouse with a background of tan chinos. She was a dreadful dresser but a wonderful therapist. In so many ways, she'd helped reunite Fortune and Jason, and he couldn't have been more grateful. Staying at Fortune's place watching TV and talking was so easy. When he came home to her after work, he felt they were becoming an "us" again.

Each week, when they came to see Dr. Chastain, they sat closer to each other, closing the gap between them on the sofa as they found their way back into each other's hearts. For Jason, Fortune had never left. She'd always had a piece of his heart, and she always would, whether this turned out to be a friendship or a marriage. He prayed that she realized that and that she was keeping his heart safe until she was ready to love again.

"Fortune and Jason, how are you today?"

"Great," they said at the same time.

They faced each other, gazes locked, unable to break away. Jason still felt the ghost of Fortune's lips on his from last week's kiss, both chaste and full of sensual promise. One day, they would get back to that cocoon of love they'd wrapped themselves in before any abysmal dinners, bad karaoke, and destroyed friendships. He was sure of it.

They'd hung out—really hung out—last week, and it wasn't just nice, it was freeing. They laughed at Dorothy and the rest of the girls, debated whether Jason was Rose or Sophia—they decided a little of both—and they ordered in a couple dozen Krispy Kremes just because they could. Between snacking on donuts and challenging each other to name the episode, they'd found their happy place again. Vivid memories of their first conversations came to him as they ate and chatted.

Before they'd met in person, they connected online just by being themselves, no filter or pretense. He'd found out she was a bit of an '80s geek with a creative side, and he confessed he loved teaching the trades, sometimes a bit more than he loved working them. Although he'd never tell his father that. No, that was only for Fortune, and so were a lot more of his quirky loves. Because she was his person, and being with his person was all that mattered now. The rest would fall into place or fall off a cliff.

Dr. Chastain scrutinized them with a quirk and a raised eyebrow. "So, what happened this past week that's got you feeling so great?"

"We hung out during a *Golden Girls* marathon." Fortune beamed.

"Okay," Dr. Chastain picked up a pad. "And this was great because ...?"

"We were just being us."

Jason chimed in. "There was no agenda, no problems to solve, no one to impress. We found out we could be together and just be us again, and it was okay." He turned to Fortune. "I think I get it now. Sometimes, trying to fix one thing leads to breaking something else. I broke us by trying to fix Seth, and I'm sorry. I—I didn't know anything. If I had … if I hadn't been so adamant about fixing things, you would have seen my heart. You would have known it was always you, and you wouldn't have had to ask. I'm sorry I made you ask."

She blinked.

He reached across the sofa for her hand and twined his fingers through hers. It was the first time since that night that he felt like they were on their way to being a couple again.

"I was supposed to be your safe space. That was what you meant about fighting for you. I not only didn't respect your opinion, I took away your safe space. Being a safe space is about trust. I know that now. It's about showing the person that you'll do anything for them because you believe in them, and you support them for who they are. I love you, and I want you to be comfortable with me again. And if that means never fixing anything again, I'll do it."

"Except the kitchen sink." She smiled.

"Not even that. I'm no plumber."

They laughed. For the first time in eons, they were happy with each other again, at least for the moment.

"I don't know how to stop being Mister Fix-it … yet. I now know why I thought I had to be, with Doctor Farragut's help, and I'm learning how to let go slowly, but I need your patience. I want us to work, and that requires me to really listen to what you have to say and to provide you a safe space. I'll do everything I can to do just that, if you can forgive me when I go into fix–it mode."

"I can forgive you for that."

"So, how do we feel about that, Fortune?" Dr. Chastain asked.

"Okay. I'm finally feeling okay." She looked up into Jason's eyes. "I forgive you. For the other stuff, too. So, can we stop talking about Seth and start working on us?"

"Yes. We can." He grabbed her hand tighter and smiled.

We're finally becoming us again.

Forty-One

Jason

"So, that was our first date." Fortune rocked back on her heels and grinned at him.

"Yeah, it was. You're not half bad for a first date." Jason chuckled.

She playfully punched him in the forearm, joining him in the laughter. "I'm the best date, period."

It wasn't their first date, of course, but it was the first since that night. The first one they'd called a date, anyway. Everything else had just been going out or had some kind of pretense. The only explanation he could give for it is that they were scared to call it a date. Doing that would cause expectations to rise, nosy friends to ask how it went, and therapists to examine and question it. Of course, that was going to happen anyway.

But she was smiling, so they'd done something right tonight. "It's so good to see you smile again." He brushed his palm over her cheek. "I've missed this. I've missed you."

"It feels good to smile again. And to date a certain handsome, geeky man again." She nudged him under his arm with her shoulder.

"I'm geeky now?"

"You kind of always were. Still sexy, though."

He wound his arms around her. "You're pretty sexy yourself."

Her face beamed with that soul-warming grin he craved. She still smiled, even though she was scarred. He marveled at that. He was just a big child, he realized now. He'd never been through anything like Fortune had. She'd lost her father, she'd been assaulted, and every day she dealt with the racism and sexism of society. How was she this strong? He was supposed to be the tough one—the big burly construction worker able to lift over a hundred pounds of rock when needed, yet he didn't have an ounce of the mental fortitude or emotional strength Fortune had. He hoped she leaned on him at least a little bit for some of that resilience.

She trailed a finger down his bicep then looked up at him. "Want to come inside?" she asked, looking up and matching his glance with coy eyes.

He knew what she was doing to him, and he was there for all of it, as the kids said. She was neither innocent nor coy. When one side of her mouth quirked up, he wanted to kiss her there just to let her know that he was on to her. "You know I do."

She turned in his arms and unlocked the door.

He didn't let her go, afraid if he did, all the juicy antic-ipation that bubbled between them would fade away. She pushed her way inside, with him holding on like a child to its mother, as if it were something they'd always done. When she turned back to him, they were in the middle of her living room, nose to nose, her breath cool and minty as it brushed his face.

He asked, "Are you sure you want this?"

"I want you."

They were the three best words she ever said besides *I love you*. He wanted to grab her and be inside her and never leave, the flood of emotion rattling through his body was that strong, but he held back. He had to take it slow. She was his precious cherry wood that couldn't be stressed or sanded incorrectly or clamped too tight, lest it be ruined. Seth had already done enough damage. The thought burned through him, causing his shoulders to clench and his fingers to curl into fists.

"Jason? Are you okay?" She rubbed his forearms until the muscles loosened.

He shook his head and then his shoulders. "I'm fine, sweetie."

"We can't let him win," she said as if she read his thoughts. "We can't let him take this from us."

He cupped her jaw with both hands. How had he gotten so lucky? This woman who should've been crumbling to pieces, afraid to trust anyone who looked like him, was standing tall, claiming him, claiming them—claiming their love and defying anyone to come between them. She wasn't a delicate piece of cherry; she was a strong, nearly unbreakable oak. He underestimated her and was in awe of her for the millionth time in the last several months.

He kissed her with a featherlight brush of his lips, teasing and tasting, before deepening the kiss and moving closer. He rubbed his thumbs back and forth against her cheeks, still protective and afraid to go too fast but wanting to touch every inch of her. He couldn't help but be protective. She had her way; this was his way of not letting anything come between them.

She wrapped her arms around his waist, leaned into him, and sighed into his mouth. Her body melted against his, the tension oozing out of her with each stroke of his tongue on hers.

He moved lower, his lips on her neck, his arms around her back, her breasts heavy against his torso, even through their clothes. Why were they even still wearing clothes? He yanked at her shirt, and she backed away enough to let him rid her of it. Underneath, the black lace-covered bra that barely held her breasts was one of his favorites. He grinned as he fingered its lace. "This for me?"

"It's for both of us."

He traced the top of one of the cups with a finger. "But it's mostly for you."

"Gotta look cute." She giggled.

That giggle never failed to calm his system. And the moan after it as he reached inside and tweaked her nipple fired him right back up again. It was like a slow burning fire from deep within him inside a tent of calm. The opposing sensations drove his need to be skin-to-skin with her.

He slid his hands down her sides. "Fortune, are you sure you want to do this?" he asked again.

"Yes, I'm sure. I need this. I need you."

He led her up her stairs. Clothes came off, caresses ramped up, and in minutes, Jason found himself adorned in only a condom and hovering over a naked, panting Fortune. He eased into her, and she tensed. He stopped to let her adjust, and she calmed. But when he sunk into her, she tensed again, this time shaking instead of panting.

His body wondered what the holdup was, but his mind was on high alert. "Sweetie, are you sure you're okay?"

"I ... I can't. I can't!" She shook her head and squirmed under him. "I want to, but I can't. Dammit, why can't I do this?" She was on the verge of tears, her gaze darting frantically in every direction.

He cupped her jaw and rubbed his thumb back and forth across her cheek, focusing her. "It's going to be fine." The corners of his mouth tipped up.

When she met his eyes, she took in a deep breath and calmed. She matched his expression, and the smooth corners of her eyes crinkled.

"I think I have an idea. Why don't we switch things up a little?" He slid an arm under her and rolled them over, so she was on top.

She gasped. When he released her, she reared back slowly, still surrounding him and taking everything in from the new vantage point. "I'm ... um ..."

He was taking it in, too. "You're beautiful."

"I was going to say self-conscious, but yours sounds better. So is a rendition of 'Love on Top' in order?" She chuckled lightly.

Jason shook his head. "I don't want Beyonce. I want you." He reached up and cradled the underside of her breast, flicking the nipple with his thumb.

She threw her head back and moaned.

"That's the song I want to hear." He moved to the other breast. "Now, I get to play with these." He weighed her breasts in his hands, each too big for his palm. He loved that about her, and he loved that he knew her in this way.

She was still self-conscious of so much of her body, the body he loved: the notches above her hips where his hands nestled perfectly and the faint ridges of stretch marks there, the curves of her soft belly that gave him more of her to touch, and that nice round ass that she swore was too flat for him to love. She had enough to grab, and he did that now, his attention shifting away from her breasts and their deliciously beaded dark brown nipples as she rocked against him.

He sat up, legs spread, lifting her as she rocked, so that when she rocked back, it was harder. He groaned in her ear, and she moaned in return, clutching his shoulders and nuzzling and kissing his neck.

If she didn't stop, she'd send him over the edge too soon.

He moved one hand from back to front, cradling her neck and urging her to meet his gaze. "Open those pretty brown eyes, sweetie," he begged. "Let me see you."

Her pupils were so blown he couldn't tell them from the brown of her irises. He slanted his lips over hers, licking hungrily into her mouth before his muscles couldn't stand it anymore, and he had to lay back.

"God, Fortune, I've wanted you like this since our second date. You feel so good." He trailed his hand down her front to where their bodies met. "Tell me what you want, Fortune."

"I ... I want more."

He circled her hood in slow, intense spirals, causing her to lift and squirm against him, the friction between them building. "More of what? Tell me." He held on to her hips and thrust up. "More of that?"

"Yes," she breathed. "Yes. More of that."

"Going to give it back to me?"

She pressed down on him, clenching him inside her, and he splayed his fingers across her back, relishing being in her and living out his fantasy.

He felt her tighten around him, and she leaned back and grabbed his thighs. She was close.

"I'm close. Jason, I'm so ..." She arched back and was gone, caught up in the waves of her fluttery peak. The fluttery orgasm meant another one was right behind. Seeing her from this angle was mesmerizing. She was a goddess—confident, sure, soaked in pleasure. She was his goddess.

He grew harder at the thought, his own orgasm building. He flipped her onto her back and stilled, waiting for her to adjust. "You okay?"

"Yes," she panted, still coming down from her high.

He wanted her to be sure, not just placating him because he needed a release. It wasn't just about healing from what Seth had done. It was about having a place to heal. They both needed a place to heal, and that place was in each other's arms. He wanted her to feel as safe there as he did. "I want to be your safe space again."

She looked surprised as the thought registered. "I *am* safe here." Her gaze filled with love and warmth, stunning him into silence. Then, she curled her legs around his lower back. "Your turn." She grinned.

"You've got another one in there." He reached between them and pressed into her. She cried out in response, legs tightening around his hips, fingernails digging into his back. "Thought so."

"You smug jerk."

"Only for you, babe." He leaned down and growled low in her ear. "Now, come for me."

They went back and forth giving, receiving, parrying, and retreating until they'd worked each other back into a feverish pitch, getting into a rhythm where they were in tandem. He breathed her in, she exhaled him out. He went deeper, and she held him inside.

He caressed her cheek. His voice was soothing but strained. "Come for me."

And she did, calling his name and arching against him.

The shudder of her orgasm went through him, and he let go then, too, his whole body vibrating with hers. He collapsed on her, their bodies a heap of entangled limbs soaked with sweat and lust.

He smiled inside. They had finally gotten past contempt, fear, and confusion and found their way back to loving each other again. It would never be like those first few months together when they were cocooned away from friends and wrapped up in each other. But that wasn't reality. This love had been tested, banged up in battle, and survived some of the worst.

And after all of that, she was still here. Their love was real.

"I love you, Fortune."

"I love you too, Jason."

A bright light shone directly in Jason's face, and he shielded his eyes to determine where it was coming from. When he spotted the askew blind, he just turned on his other side and snuggled against his goddess. Last night, she'd gone from frightened to riding him like a cowgirl. Was her being on top of him fixing things? At the time, it was his selfish wish fulfillment, but he'd wanted to make sure she saw it as a suggestion, one she could take or leave. Boy, was he glad she took it, though.

"Are you watching me sleep again? That's kinda creepy, you know." She chuckled softly, reaching behind her and caressing his cheek.

"Stop being this beautiful in the morning, and I'll stop staring." He trailed a hand down her arm, over her side, to between her legs. It didn't take long to work her to writhing and panting. He slid on a condom, and they tried another new position for them. With her leg bent over him, her butt in his lap, he wasn't sure how this was even better than his fantasy, but it was.

After they cleaned up and returned to snuggling together in bed, they planned their schedules, imagining the rest of their lives together. Well, at least the next few weeks. Fortune's fortieth was only a month away, and now that they were together again, Jason had no idea how she wanted to celebrate.

"So, what do you want to do for your birthday? Group date, right?" He laughed softly near her ear.

"Um, no. You know better than that. How about a group party instead?"

"That sounds like a good idea."

She reached for her phone on the nightstand, unlocked it, and opened her contact list. "Here. Invite only the people in the 'Cool Geeks' list." A text came in from Louis. "Gotta meet him for lunch." She headed for the bathroom. "Only the cool geeks!" she sang back at him.

When he heard the shower cut on, he quickly scrolled through the contacts until he found the one he was looking for and sent it to his phone.

After they parted, he rushed home. For some reason, he was compelled to make the call in the confines of his place and not the car, so he wouldn't have to multitask. He dialed the number from Fortune's contacts and waited, hoping the end party would pick up.

An alto that sounded a lot like Fortune answered.

"Hello? Mrs. Edwards? This is Jason Reed. I believe Fortune told you about me. Yes. I know this may seem out of the blue, but I'd like to ask for your blessing to marry her."

Epilogue

THE WEEKEND AFTER FORTUNE'S 40th birthday, Jason was running around his townhouse like a wild man, moving furniture, directing deliveries, and asking Dani why all the decorations she'd bought were black and gray.

"It's a fortieth birthday! You're officially over the hill."

"But Fortune's already been through enough doom and gloom. Weren't there some decorations in a happy color?"

"Not that said happy fortieth."

Jason sighed, exasperated that none of his friends could improvise.

Ranjan walked in with the birthday cake, Darren in tow. "The cake has arrived, and it's delicious!"

Jason gaped in horror. "You ate part of the cake?"

Ranjan laughed. "No! It looks delicious, doesn't it?" He set it on the kitchen counter away from stray elbows. "Jason, you seem stressed. Have a seat." He escorted Jason to a seat in his own armchair. "It's going to be great. She's going to love it. You know why? Because she loves you."

Ranjan was right. Fortune would be happy no matter what color the streamers were, or if the cake wasn't perfect—which it was, thank you very much—because she'd be surrounded by friends. Hers and his.

"Thanks, Ranjan."

"Thank you for bringing this wonderful woman into our lives. We really do like her. And I like her for you. You're less emo when she's around."

Jason shoved his long-time friend, and they laughed. Ranjan's words soothed Jason. If he hadn't been sure before, he was now. His friends had come around. And not because he fixed anything, but because she was his person, and everyone saw it.

"Happy birthday to me!" Fortune was in the front doorway, still open from the last person who entered. Louis and Celeste were behind her.

Jason ran, grabbed her waist, and twirled her around in his arms. "Happy Birthday, sweetie."

Someone turned the music up louder, and everyone went into party mode—pouring drinks, gathering around the couple, and dancing.

After about a half hour, someone cut out the lights, darkening the room except for four candles on the cake and several cell phone screens.

"Happy birthday, sweetie." Jason held the cake steady in front of her while she blew out the candles.

The lights came up on a room full of Fortune's friends surrounding her, cheering and clapping. The cheering segued into Stevie Wonder's rendition of "Happy Birthday" while

Jason placed the cake on the island and led her to the center of the room where the living room furniture had been pushed back to create a makeshift dance floor.

"I thought you didn't dance, Mr. Reed."

"I can make an exception for a certain person's fortieth birthday. Just don't ask me to be your DanceMania partner." He laughed.

"Oh, no. That's always Celeste."

Fortune fell into step and laughed with him, and he was even more certain that she was his person. He scanned the room and saw her friends and family talking and laughing with his as if this were more of a reunion than when most of these people first met, and that could only bode well for the future. The wedding would be an even bigger, more jovial party. Of course, he'd have to convince her to have an open bar.

"Happy Birthday, little sis." A tall guy with dark brown skin and more than a slight resemblance to Fortune walked up to them.

When she saw him, she squealed and stopped mid dance to give him a hug. "Kendal! I haven't seen you in ages!"

"Girl, I just saw you last month. You asked me to change the oil in your car." Kendal rolled his eyes but hugged his sister back, anyway.

"And you didn't even stick around to taste the baked chicken I made!" She turned to Jason. "Kendal, this is my boyfriend, Jason. Jason, this is my brother Kendal. How did you know to invite him? He's not on my 'cool geeks' list. He's just a regular geek."

A smug smile emerged on Jason's face. "I just thought maybe you'd want to celebrate with family and friends."

"Mom sends her love, by the way. And she needs to talk to you after this." He threw a blank look at Jason. "Take care of my sister, dude, or I'm coming after you." He burst into a full-face grin. "Nice meeting you. Thanks for inviting me." He shook Jason's hand and then melted into the crowd of people hovering around the island, which was now a self-service bar, apparently.

Jason stared wide-eyed at Fortune. "Should I be scared?"

She nodded. "Definitely. He's serious." She grinned. "But you'd have to do something really horrendous to warrant an attack like that. Like forcing me to go on a series of group dates with your friends."

"You're not going to let me live that down, are you?"

"Nope." She leaned in and kissed him slowly, and party-goers who noticed whooped and hollered.

The night wound down, and the guests trickled out of the townhouse as Lyft rides arrived. Graham, Dani, Louis, Celeste, and Mauricio stayed to help Jason and Fortune clean up.

"You've got a good one, Reed." Graham nodded in Fortune's direction. She, Dani, and Celeste were in the kitchen laughing and talking.

Pride and happiness swelled in Jason's chest, and he silently thanked whatever God was listening for getting them to this moment. Everything was going to be alright. "Yeah, I know."

"Planning to keep her?"

Jason patted his pants pocket. "If she says yes."

Graham smiled and patted him on the back. "That's what I'm talking about." He checked his phone. "Our ride's here. You good?"

Jason clasped his best friend in a bro hug. "Perfect. Thanks for coming. And for everything else."

"What are friends for? Dani!" When she glanced up, Graham signaled to the door. "Our ride's here. Night all!"

Louis and Mauricio came in from dumping trash outside. "Y'all ready?" Louis asked Celeste and Mauricio. He was their designated driver since he had an early morning preparing for this year's Alzheimer's gala. They nodded, and everyone said their goodbyes.

Jason ushered them out, then turned back to Fortune and exhaled. "What a party." He crossed the room and gave her a light kiss on the cheek.

"Yeah, what a party. I haven't had that much fun in ages." She kissed him back. "Thank you for that."

"Was happy to do it. You know I'd do anything to see you smile."

"Although ... there was one thing missing."

He raised his eyebrows. "What's that?"

She smirked and leaned back against the kitchen island. "Celeste and Louis thought you were going to propose."

Jason pulled a little blue box out of his pocket. "Well, it just so happens I have another present for you."

Fortune's eyes went as wide as saucers as she straightened. "What are you—"

He stepped closer to her and grasped her hands. "We've been through a lot this year, more than I ever thought we'd have to go through, especially this soon in our relationship. You stood by me, but you also challenged me to examine myself and my situation, and you forced me to make some hard but necessary choices. It's a rare goddess who takes time to bring someone down to earth, but thanks for doing that. And you did it at the expense of your emotional health. So, now it's time for me to support you."

He went down on one knee, while still keeping a firm hold on her hands.

He released her hands only for a moment to open the blue box and reveal a shiny diamond and platinum ring. His heart swelled with warm pride and something so strong it almost bowled him over.

This is why people get down on one knee when they do this.

"Fortune Edwards, I love you so much. Will you do me the honor of being my wife?"

Fortune stood silently as if she were frozen.

"Fortune?" He shook the fingers of her left hand. The diamond glinted as the light bounced off it. It was so bright, so perfect. Just like she was.

"Yes?" She was staring so hard at the ring that he wondered if he'd picked the right one.

"Um ..."

Then her eyes lit with awareness. "Oh! Yes."

"Yes?"

"Yes, I'll marry you!" She laughed.

He jumped up and swept her into his arms, so happy he could burst.

Do you want more of Jason and Fortune's love story? Or maybe you identified with Jason and Graham's gaming or Fortune's geekiness about 80s TV and movies? Be a Nerdy Romantics newsletter subscriber and get your nerdy and romance urges fulfilled.

The Nerdy Romantics newsletter is a monthly newsletter packed with book recs, first looks, a little about me, and behind-the-scenes podcast episode info with links to show notes.

Sign up and get "THE SETH CHAPTERS", bonus chapters from *The Accidental Proposal* from Seth's point of view. Go to https://ymnelson.com/bonus-content or scan the QR code below to sign up!

Sneak Peek

While this series is totally fiction, the first book was inspired by my real-life experimental dating on Tinder, which I documented on my blog. (If you missed it, check out #MyTinderSeries https://ymnelson.com/category/mytinder-series/)

Because readers really responded to the series, it inspired me to write a fictional what-if story that ended in an HEA. And *The Accidental Swipe* was born.

This is why reviews are so important. They tell other readers about great books, and they tell us authors what you really liked (which can inspire more books you want).

So, please review *The Accidental Proposal* wherever you bought your copy, Goodreads, and BookBub.

Read on for a sneak peek of the last book in the Accidental Lovers series, *The On Purpose Wedding!*

The On Purpose Wedding

Fortune and Jason at the Church

Fortune stood in the center aisle of the sanctuary wondering if lightning would indeed strike her for the nasty thoughts she was having. Jason was at the front of the church, standing on the second step of the semicircular dais talking with the pastor about some nitpicky details he thought were critical to choosing this as the church he would get married in. As if they could change the dark stain on the oak pews or repaint the walls gray instead of the bright beige that took away from the Victorian-style interior.

She couldn't care less.

Who knew he would be such a Groomzilla?

No, she wasn't imagining him naked. Those types of naughty thoughts were for when he wasn't asking a pastor if they could attach bouquets to the end of pews. This fantasy was more the revenge kind wherein Jason cursed out Marshall Li-Schneider, then decked him in front of a jaw-dropped, saucer-size-eyed congregation. The vision horrified her, but it also made her a little giddy, too. It would be like knocking down all the evils of her past love life so they could enter a new life together.

After Jason's former friend Seth was convicted of assaulting her and sentenced to a whopping five years in prison (three if he stayed on good behavior), Fortune was certain that at least their engagement would be drama-free.

She was riding a wave of delusion that day.

Someone told Jason's ex-fiancée Lily about their engagement, so Lily put a bug in Jason's ear about being sure he wanted to get married, or something like that. He'd been vague on their conversation, but after that, he went from zero to obsessive with making sure every single preparation was perfect.

So much for being drama-free.

Lily's goal might've been to make Jason question their nuptials, but what she'd really done, aside from putting Jason into wedding overdrive, was make Fortune think about exes and what-ifs, and her biggest what-if was Marshall. The crush-turned-bully who rated her a four-and-a-half in high school. Luckily, she hadn't seen or heard from Marshall since they graduated, and since they didn't have friends in common, she doubted he would even hear about her engagement. And while she shouldn't have cared less about that thought, it made her feel slightly bummed—like she wished she could show Marshall someone thought she was so desirable they wanted to marry her.

He probably wouldn't even care anyway. It wasn't as if Marshall actually liked her in high school. She'd had a crush, and he'd been a teenage boy with teenage boy level hormones, taking advantage of a hopeful girl in a good mood. As soon as she'd realized he was using her, she pushed him away, so he retaliated by insulting her and rating her a four and a half. She'd let that dictate her dating life ever since, until Jason showed her how wrong that thinking was.

Marshall wasn't even thinking about her. Probably hadn't given her a second thought since high school. He certainly would not meddle in her wedding. She shook away the thoughts and joined Jason and the pastor.

"Sweetie?" Jason pulled her snug against his side. "Do you have questions for Reverend Campbell?"

The warmth and tightness of his embrace shot an arrow of comfort in between her shoulders, and that bummed feeling disappeared. She shook her head and smiled up at him. "I think you've asked enough questions for the both of us."

"Well, if you think of anything else, don't hesitate to call me." The slight pastor handed Jason a business card. Next to Jason, Reverend Campbell barely came up to his shoulder. "And remember to give yourself enough time to go through all the marriage counseling sessions. I won't perform a wedding without my couples getting counseling."

"Yes, sir." Jason smiled, sticking out his free hand to shake Reverend Campbell's, seeming to swallow the small man's hand in his own. "We'll be in touch soon."

The pastor nodded and returned Jason's smile. "You make a beautiful couple. Congratulations to both of you. Please stay as long as you like." He ran a hand through his thinning brown hair then headed to his office, leaving the couple hugged up and staring at the pulpit.

Fortune glanced at Jason briefly, then stared in the direction of where the pastor went. "What are you thinking?"

"I'm thinking that this wedding is going to cost a fortune, Fortune." He laughed at his not quite funny joke, and the bellow echoed throughout the sanctuary.

She groaned. "That wasn't funny. How much is this one?"

"Five hundred more than the last one. But this is the one I like. Do you like it?"

She shrugged. "Sure," she said absently.

He turned, wrapping his other arm around her and squeezing. He bent his head, eyebrows furrowed but lips turned up at the corners. "Are you lying?"

She stared up into his eyes, the pools of blue darkening to indigo. He was worried or angry. She hoped it was the former. Fortune flattened her palm against his back and stroked up and down, hoping the action would calm him. "I'm not lying. I do like it. But I also liked the last one and the one before that. A church is a church. Reverend Campbell's super nice, though."

"Am I being picky?"

She held up her hand, her thumb and index finger not quite touching. "A tad bit, yes." She smiled. "You're almost Groomzilla level at this point."

"For real?" Jason frowned, eyebrows furrowed. He let go of her and gazed around the room, his shoulders slumped and back rounded. Her defeated giant. "I thought I was chill."

She raised her eyebrows and blew a raspberry. "You were at first. But now you're somewhere in between Regine Hunter from *Living Single* and Miranda Priestly in *The Devil Wears Prada.* I've never seen you like this. I thought Louis was bad, but you've got him beat."

The lines on his forehead deepened as he doubled down on his frown. He looked at his shoes. Had he broken so early in the planning process? They hadn't even met each other's parents yet. They'd both called her mom and then his mom and dad, and both calls had gone well. But a real sit down? No. If he couldn't pick out a ceremony venue without getting this worked up, he was going to go to pieces when they sat down with her family.

He leaned away from her and against a pew. "I didn't think I'd gotten that bad already. I guess I got worked up after Lily found out."

She wasn't going to mention it, but since he had, she couldn't let it slide. She backed away as well, bending her head to keep his gaze. "What did Lily say to you exactly?"

"Just that I needed to redeem myself from when we were engaged. That I needed to be sure I was getting married for the right reasons."

She huffed. "Sounds like she's not in our corner."

He shook his head. "She always thought I asked her because I was feeling like I needed to win ... at ...I don't know. Win at weddings or something. What guy wants to be the first of his friends to get married?"

"This is probably not a great time to point this out, but you are the first of your friends to get married." She raised her eyebrows.

He looked up at the ceiling. "Oh yeah. You're right." He shook his head. "She's just trying to meddle, anyway. She likes drama."

Fortune laughed, and it echoed off the sanctuary's walls. "As if we haven't had enough of that."

He hauled himself off the pew and pulled her into his embrace. "Sweetie, I'm sorry about all of this. First Seth, and now Lily. I don't want to lose you. We can't let these people get in the way of our happiness."

She lay her head on his chest, his heat warming her cheek. Everything was right in the world when she was here. "You won't lose me, Jason Reed. I love you too much."

Be notified when this book is available for pre-order: https://ymnelson.com/bob-signups

AUTHOR'S NOTE

One of the first scenes of this story I saw was the *black moment*. It disturbed me so much, I didn't want to write it. But what disturbed me even more was that a former American presidential candidate talked about doing this very thing to a woman, and people—WOMEN—voted for him. It bothered me because those very same women were disgusted by the morality of another former American president and wanted him removed from office.

That got me thinking about traits that people overlook in people they root for that they wouldn't overlook in others. Sometimes beliefs and hope blind people to facts and logic. (As a Trekkie and someone who loves Spock, it baffles me.) In an episode of the TV show *Queen Sugar*, Nova asks her white boyfriend if he felt shame for what cops had done to George Floyd. It's that lack of a collective consciousness among certain groups of people that ultimately doom them.

In the end, women ended up protesting this so-called president for most of his first year in office—the president they voted for despite what he said he did to get women's attention. Four years of destruction, division, and chaos (not to mention installing lifetime-appointed judges who would take away these same women's reproductive rights) could have been prevented if women had actually listened to what this man was saying and made an objective choice instead of voting based on some arbitrary belief system and turning a blind eye because they felt they had the privilege to do so.

And in the end, I had to write about it. I knew that I would possibly get backlash for that scene, or that it would make people angry or disgusted. If so, then good. You should be. But you should have been angry and disgusted in 2016. How dare someone talk about a woman in that manner and get any woman's vote.

This book is not about politics. (To be clear: racism is not politics. It's a system of social oppression and discrimination. It's societal cancer.) But it is partly about the pain and grief we could prevent if we just look at a situation and a person objectively, just for a moment, and make a better, more logical decision about them. And about ourselves.

Playlist

1. "Feels" by Ed Sheeran (featuring Young Thug & J Hus)

2. "Mercy" by Shawn Mendes

3. "Us" by James Bay

4. "I Am a Black Woman" by Chewii

5. "Human" by Rag'n'Bone Man

6. "High Horse" by Kacey Musgraves

7. "Unfair" by Rayana Jay

8. "Give In To Me" by Michael Jackson

9. "Wall" by James Droll

10. "Circles" by Post Malone

11. "Birds" by Imagine Dragons

12. "Graveyard" by Halsey

13. "You Can't Save Me" by SiR

14. "Let Me Go (Mav's Version)" by Maverick Sabre

15. "Blackout" by Dahlia Sleeps

16. "Black Woman" by Danielle Brooks

17. "Floods" by Lucky Daye

18. "Keep Your Head Child (Demo)" by JNR WILLIAMS

19. "Thin Air" by Colouring

20. "Right Here Waiting" by Richard Marx

21. "Let Me Hold You" by Nick Wilson

22. "You" by Alex Condliffe & Lamb Hands

23. "1961" by The Fray

24. "Something Better" by Minke

25. "Friends" by Ella Henderson

26. "Adore You" by Harry Styles

27. "Simple Things" by Miguel

28. "The Few Things" by JP Saxe

Listen to *The Accidental Proposal* playlist on Spotify

Acknowledgements

This time around, I was hesitant to show this book to any-one. I had to get it out of my head, but who would get it? Like really get it? Thankfully, my beta readers Gracey E. and Saword E. were there to give thoughtful feedback, and in some areas, confirm what I hesitated to think myself—that this was a story that needed to be told and might even be thought about after the last page. And isn't that what most writers want?

Thanks to my editor Suanne S. who gave me great insight, especially on the assault scene that made the story move where I was afraid to take it and my proofreader Victoria S. who made it shine (and taught me some about valium!). Thanks also to my cover designer Amber D. who completely redid the cover when I realized the tone of the story was different than I thought it would be (see her previous work on the bonus chapters for this book).

My friends and family have been so supportive of me as a writer that I wonder why I didn't start doing this earlier. Thanks Dana, Millard, Marcie, Staci, Pam, Peggy, Bethanie, Laura, John, and so many more of you that I can't name in this limited space.

Mom, I love that you insisted on getting the first copy of *The Accidental Swipe* even though I wanted to trade it for a better looking one. I promise this first one will look better. Bro, thanks for just being you, opinions and all.

Most of all thanks to the fans of Jason, Fortune, Owen, Makayla, and all of the other imaginary characters I put to paper. You keep me writing. Well, you and coffee.

About the Author

Y.M. Nelson is based in Charlotte, NC and writes about love, women's journeys, and amateur DIY. After she spent most of her writing "career" ghostwriting for companies, Y. M. decided to produce and share her own work with the public. Her debut romantic comedy *The Accidental Swipe* is based on her #MyTinderSeries blog serial. When she's not writing, Y. M. hosts the Nerdy Romantics Podcast which she created. She can also be found teaching college English, baking something sweet, upcycling random pieces of furniture, or watching reruns from one of the *Star Trek* franchises.

Follow her at https://ymnelson.com for the latest news and links to her social media.

𝖆

amazon.com/stores/Y.-M.-Nelson/author/B01MUAO9A5

BB

bookbub.com/authors/y-m-nelson

g

goodreads.com/ymnelson

f

facebook.com/authorymnelson

𝓟

pinterest.com/authorymnelson

instagram.com/authorymnelson

Printed in the USA
CPSIA information can be obtained
at www.ICGtesting.com
LVHW041303300624
784213LV00005B/20